# Strangers On a Coach

*Della Mason*

Travelogue Publications, UK

First published in Great Britain in 2001 by
Travelogue Publications
PO Box 3751, Bournemouth, BH1 1YJ

Copyright © 2001 Della Mason

ISBN 0-9540738-0-0
Printed by Antony Rowe Ltd, Chippenham, Wilts, UK
Cover produced by Evergreen Graphics, Aldwick, West Sussex, UK

For the coach drivers,
unsung heroes of our busy roads,
whose skill & good humour we rely upon.

*Special thanks to my family: Felicity, my editor throughout; Richard, who did the graphics, and Julia and James for all their help and encouragement.*

*My added thanks to Edinburgh and Lothians Tourist Board and to the Scottish Tourist Board, Inverness, for their wonderful enthusiasm.*

*Whenever help was needed they were all there with the answers.*

D.M.

*Useful Internet sites*

For researching your Scottish family records.
**General Register Office for
Scotland, Edinburgh**
 **www.origins.net**  (births,deaths,
marriages) Births and marriages from 1553.
Some 28 million names, making this one of
the world's largest resources of genealogical
information.

**Edinburgh & Lothians Tourist Board,**
Edinburgh, for full tourist information,
events, travel, accommodation
**www.edinburgh.org**

**The Woollen Mill,** The Royal Mile,
Edinburgh
**www.woollenmill.co.uk**
Tartans, clan crests, kilts, cashmeres
(world postal service)

# Strangers On a Coach

# CHAPTER ONE

## Heading North

It reminded me of highwaymen. I could feel the Scarborough coaching inn's sinister past. Yet here we were tucked up for the night, warm and cosy; too cosy I thought.

I could be sleeping in Nell Gwyn's bed or maybe Queen Elizabeth I had slept here. The huge old four poster with its crisp cotton covered duvet and frilled drapes above me, would have amazing secrets.

I decided I would get a guide book in the morning.

Just then I heard a tap-tapping on the door. At 1.15am who could it be?

Possibly Jill, who sat beside me on the coach from London.

Sneaking forward I listened and waited. But there was no sound.

'Is that you, Jill?' I whispered.

There was no reply.

I decided to try the door handle, to make sure it was locked. But it wasn't. It sprang open and before me stood a man dressed head to toe in a suit of armour. He was smiling broadly.

I stood looking for a full half minute, amazed that it wasn't Jill, not too sure who it was, yet, oddly not scared at all.

I didn't speak. I could not think of the right thing to say but I didn't keel over in terror either. In some strange way he seemed perfectly in keeping with the place. I half smiled and gently closed the door and put the latch across, then locked it too.

After that I slept well. It somehow seemed just right having such a stalwart champion standing guard at my door. It brought all the history of the old King Charles Inn, to life.

Next morning when Ted Webster, our coach driver, said in his breezy way 'Well, did anyone see any ghosts?' I piped up 'There was a man in a suit of armour who knocked on my bedroom door.'

We were already all aboard the coach heading North along the M1, towards Scotland.

Suddenly everyone turned, in one movement, to look round at me, as if I said I had just won ten million on the lottery. Ted started to talk excitedly over the microphone 'You really saw a man in armour?'

'Why yes, he was standing outside my bedroom door.'

'Oh my god' said the slim tough-looking American from Texas, opposite, with delight. 'You saw a man in armour, I wish you had called me.'

Suddenly I was the centre of attention. Even Jill, by my

side, was nudging me.  'Are you  certain Amy, that you weren't dreaming?'

I nodded.   Of course  I was sure. 'Next time it happens I'll shout for help' I said  quite loudly.

'That was  the  ghost' said Ted, as he drove  in his expert way.   He revved the engine to go faster.

'That was  *the ghost*.'

There was a  hush  throughout the coach. No one  said a word. What did Ted mean?   That was 'the ghost.' I made a mental note to ask him later.  Was it an  omen?

'Where are we staying tonight?' asked  a female voice at the  front of the coach.

Someone on the far side, said    'Edinburgh.' And it all went silent again.

'Any ghosts there?' asked the Texan.

'Aye.. millions'  a  dour Scots accent  burled across the coach.

You  could  feel  the  intensity  and  the  excitement mounting. It was as though someone  had said we were going to  lunch on  the moon that day.  It was sharp and real, yet almost unreal too. Suddenly the  holiday tour took on a whole new perspective. Two days ago I did not believe in ghosts.  Now  I  had seen one.

'Weren't you a bit frightened?' said Jill, munching into a  choc bar, and  offering me one.

'No, I thought he was real.'

At that she  squeaked with delight.

The coach party settled into a warmth of quiet chatter as people talked across seats and laughter rang out and we began to get to know each other.

We were now glimpsing the wide rolling Northumbrian countryside that stretched like a green and gold patchwork around us.

On the A68 the road went over hills that seemed to reach forever into the distance. Ted told us that on a clear day from here you could see across the width of England - to the sparkling blue seas on either side.

He probably sensed that no-one quite believed this because two miles further on, he pulled the coach onto a parking spot and said with a flourish 'Here we are. We'll stretch our legs and you can get a few pictures. You can see the North Sea behind us and over there the Atlantic Ocean.'

It was true. England seemed rather small. Now we really felt like an island.

Cameras click-clicked. People looked and some chatted. The tall lady with large blue sparkly eyes and her hair swathed into a tousled bun at her nape, smiled then introduced herself in an engaging American accent. 'Hello, I'm Dolly Whitby, sitting just ahead of you. What an amazing view this is.'

I nodded agreement and took her outstretched hand.

'I'm Amy Billington, nice to meet you.' A crisp breeze whistled over our heads.

Jill was admiring the vast vista that stretched before us into infinity. Trees and fields fell away into the far beyond. It was like a painting. Or like sitting on top of the world. The sun and clouds highlighted the view, bringing colours into sharp focus.

'Your first visit?' I asked Dolly and she nodded with a warm smile.

I knew that before long we would all be chatting like old friends. That was the fun of coaching.

Dolly hugged her jacket about her as the strong breeze swept over the hills towards us. It was bright, fresh and very cool, especially after the warmth of the coach. It was a wind that you felt had travelled all the way from Canada or the United States.

'I'm here to see if I can locate my ancestors.' she said.

'Scottish are they?' I half gasped.

A delighted and rather proud grin lit up her face. 'Yes, we're MacGregors'

Jill was agog at this. 'Rob Roy's clan!'

Dolly looked amazed and delighted at such instant reference. 'You mean we could be related?'

'Well he's the most famous MacGregor of all' added Jill, quite forgetting to say that he was also the most infamous. But that, I thought, could come later if Dolly wanted the whole turbulent story. Soon they were chatting and Jill was offering to lend her a clan book that she had brought along.

Two more minutes and Ted was making for the coach and indicating that the 'pit stop' was over.

As I turned to get on board, beside me stood a man with a small cape wrapped sensibly and quite elegantly around his shoulders. He had a curious look about him resembling Sherlock Holmes. I smiled to myself: all he needed was a pipe to complete the picture. He certainly had a remarkably intelligent face.

He could almost have been 'Holmes' heading back to Scotland, to solve a mystery as he so often did, leaving behind his London rooms and the now famous address in Baker Street.

'Holmes' got on the coach ahead of me. Or rather he was about to and then must have noticed how impolite it was, and stepped aside with a flourish of his arm. He was wearing the most expensive pigskin handstitched gloves. Obviously he was not used to scrimping on the finer things in life.

I nodded a swift 'thank you', climbed aboard and found my seat.

Ted was already busily counting 'his sheep', half under his breath glancing around the seats, making quite sure the party was again complete.

'What did you think of that view?' he said moving the coach up a gear as we sped away.

Everyone murmured appreciatively.

'Thought you'd like it. We're heading well North now.

'We'll soon be    crossing   over the Border into Scotland.'

The coach purred along as we started to chatter happily to our neighbours.    All that marvellous fresh air. Here we were far away from the traffic chaos of the South of England, starting at last to relax, finding open roads and scenery that stretched beyond merely the next corner.

The enchantment of a tour that would lead us to the Highlands of Scotland was already with me and as I heard voices and merriment at the rear of the coach I suspected that the magic was beginning to work for all of us.

We would be in Edinburgh before nightfall, into a world where culture and tradition meant something entirely different.    And I was with a coach party of people from many different countries, who already, though I hardly knew them yet, seemed unusual and interesting.

# CHAPTER TWO

## *An Edinburgh welcome*

The sky rolled like a blanket over us and the rain clouds gathered. We were hoping to make Edinburgh before dark, though the shafts of light were dwindling fast.

I had already - in past times - seen Edinburgh in stormy, icy and snowy weather. And every one of them left a different impression of enchantment. Even if at times, I had had to rush to buy long boots or heavyweight tights.

But this was August. It was summertime. The weather would be good and the city alive with thousands of Festival visitors.

I had one eye taking in the scenery of sheer cliffs near Berwick-Upon-Tweed and the sea rolling and crashing far, far below. I loved this part of the A1 where the main road runs alongside the North Sea and the wild uninhabited countryside gives us a glimpse of delights yet to come. I could hear too the gasps of other passengers. Some were coming over from the far side, tempted to see the beauty that we were all enjoying.

'We could be in Edinburgh by nine' said Jill, putting down a book she had been studying.

I smiled and nodded.

'We'll be ravenous by then.'

'Aye.'

'You'll be taking up the local language' I joked.

'Only if I ken.'

At that I burst into a fit of giggles.

'You *are* doing well. Is that a Scots dictionary by any chance?'

'It has some 'most used' words. I thought they might be useful. 'ken means know.' She turned the pages gently. 'Here we are : 'do ye' ken' means 'do you know''

Dolly, her face appearing from the side of the seat in front, said 'I find Edinburrg-h a confusing word. I keep getting it wrong.' She had obviously overheard our discussion and was keen to get some tips.

Jill rose to the bait. She flicked through her book then read aloud. 'Edinburgh: pronounced Ed-in-burr. You put the accent on the second part and forget the g and the h. Just remember to say 'Ed - in- burr..rrr.'

As we practised aloud everyone began to join in. The coach buzzed with repetitions of the city's famous name.

Ted heard the commotion and laughed. 'What about Auchterarder?'

Everyone had a go. Then we exploded in merriment, most people forgetting how tired they were, as the new

9

Scottish place name rolled off their tongues, giving them the 'feel' for the country they were about to explore.

'What time do we arrive Ted ?' asked a female voice from the far back of the coach.

'Another hour unless the rain comes down in buckets' he quipped.

Someone started singing gently the Harry Lauder song, The Road To The Isles. It was joined by nearly everyone and swelled like an anthem.

> 'For *you* take the high road
> and *I'll* take the low road..
> and I'll be in Scotland 'afore ye.'

As the tune faded away everyone cheered gently. We were in fine spirits and the coach party, though we all hardly knew each other yet and had only spoken mostly to colleagues sitting beside us, had melded into a warmth that felt comforting: we were collectively a party that knew how to enjoy ourselves. It was certain this would be a fine tour. I could almost feel it in my bones.

Jill was speaking quietly into my left ear. 'We're staying in Inverleith. About one mile from Princes Street, I've been looking it up on the city map.'

I glanced over at the map she had folded and propped up on the small table that perched out from the seat in front, aircraft style.

Four star. The Deerstalker. 'That's a strange name for a hotel in the centre of Edinburgh.'

She nodded. And was lost in thought, and reading up on her local history again.

'Gosh. Famous people have dined there. Robert Louis Stevenson, Sir Arthur Conan Doyle and some well known Scots poets. And they have spectacular Burns nights on January 25. Aah.. Rabbie Burns.'

The nice thing I quickly learned about Jill was that she didn't necessarily require me to answer. She just carried on talking, imparting very useful and knowledgeable pieces of information and was content that I was listening.

Jill is a teacher in a large senior school just outside Basingstoke. Her main subject is English and she also does modern history, which over the years has become a great passion. Her Scottish jaunt is to get some real input for a project she plans with her GCSE and 'A' and 'AS' level students. What a good teacher she must be, I thought. She was a mine of information, all being revealed at the right moment to catch our interest, like showers of gold dust.

The unspoken thought we shared was that we were probably expected to know all about Scotland.

Foreigners on this journey had the quite mammoth job of trying to assimilate Scotland in eight days! They would want to go home packed with knowledge and tales, so that when they showed their photos and videos, they had amazing stories to tell.

Dolly, our American, was asking Jill a question. They had already formed a good bond.

'Is Edinburgh really as pretty as its pictures?'

'More beautiful, if anything, isn't it Amy?' said Jill, turning to me.

'Yes, it's stunning.' I smiled broadly, remembering the overwhelming welcomes I'd always received there. 'It's very friendly and lively.'

Dolly looked pleased and full of anticipation.

Outside the wide windows the passing scenery was fading into the darkness. We had left the coastline. Road signs were beginning to say: EDINBURGH.

'Holmes' had moved seats and was sitting almost opposite. He leaned across.

'I wonder if you know anything about the hotel where we are staying? Is it historic or modern?'

His eyebrows were well formed and his hair held only hints of grey at the temples. With his golden tan and slim features he was, I thought, an attractive man.

Jill responded by searching for her hotel guide and handing it to him. 'Here we are, sounds very interesting. Sir Arthur Conan Doyle once frequented the dining rooms.'

A broad grin lit his normally serious face. He took the booklet. 'May I?'

'Yes, of course' Jill smiled. And looked sideways at me.

'Lots to interest you in Edinburgh if you're keen on Conan Doyle. I'm Jill, by the way.' She held out her hand as she spoke, taking him by surprise. He gripped it, slightly shyly I thought.

'Watson, John Watson' he quickly added 'not Dr Watson, I'm afraid. I belong to the London Sherlock Holmes Society. I thought I'd escape up here to pick up a bit of atmosphere, you could say.'

'You must know all his works?'

'Well, I like to think so but we're always discovering new bits and pieces you know.'

'Yes, of course.'

He turned to start reading the booklet and Jill half smiled. She knew I had heard the conversation.

So I was right. He was a Holmes sleuth. I could now call him either Sherlock Holmes. Or, in truth, Mr Watson.

I was feeling quite pleased with the way things were working out.

I even dared to think what an intriguing bunch of tourists we had collected on board. It augured well for the days ahead.

Ahead of us, seated next to Dolly, was Heidi, a former dancer, now in her early sixties, who was hoping to revive a few friendships in Scotland. She had brought a host of telephone numbers with her.

I could hear from her talk and laughter with Dolly that they were getting on famously. She sounded vivacious;

full of fun. Her hair was swept up in an unusual version of a French pleat; rather higher I would say. Her nails I had noticed, when we had coffee, were finely manicured, and painted deep red.

She wore sensible yet dramatic clothes for travelling; deep magenta velvet stretch trousers, with a stunning lambswool top in fuchsia, and a chiffon scarf. You could see that she was 'show biz'; quite definitely.

The rest of us were in far duller outfits. I stuck to my trouser suit, in medium beige, with a white polo top.

And Dolly was in a pink shirt and well cut trousers. They looked expensive, very American and quite conservative.

Jill, in her mid-40's, with short cropped dark hair and twinkling dark brown eyes, was in separates: a pale blue top with a matching cardigan; one of the current favourites with professionals. Jill wore it with a quite long slim navy skirt, looking every inch the teacher, yet very fashionable.

It was just then that Texan Don Oldenshaw appeared in the gangway. He nodded and smiled in his friendly way and held his camera aloft. 'Just taking a shot of us all together in the coach .'

'Handy in case one of us ever gets lost' I quipped.

He did not take this seriously. But I had a feeling that if he wasn't snapping us with his camera, he would invariably be cine-filming. However no one minded. Maybe he was planning to make a film. And we were all the stars.

Ted's microphone crackled into action. And everyone listened.

'We'll be heading into Edinburgh in about fifteen minutes. We'll go in along the historic Royal Mile. That way we may see part of the Festival Tattoo as we arrive. Then we'll drive down The Mound towards Princes Street. It's a magnificent view.'

Everyone listened intently. We could tell that Ted knew his Edinburgh.

There was a general murmur of excitement from all corners of the coach.

Now it was dark and we were rushing through the countryside at a good speed. The thought of our imminent arrival had its effect on the passengers.

In front Dolly turned round excitedly 'This is the moment I've been waiting for ever since I was eight years old.' Her face glowed with the expectancy of it all.

Jill, beside me, was moving from side to side as though she too was wide awake with anticipation. 'Coming in when it's dark - and in the middle of the Festival Tattoo. I've never done that before. It's quite amazing, isn't it?'

I agreed totally. It was dramatic timing. No one entering the city in this way was ever likely to forget it.

Any slight tinge of tiredness we were feeling, following the long drive, evaporated. We were just like a crowd of schoolchildren, curious, aware, almost too excited to speak.

Within minutes the coach seemed to be into suburban Edinburgh.

Streets changed from those with tidy front gardens and stone walls, and curtain drapes to shop fronts and smaller, narrower high rise tenements. Occasionally one would get a glimpse inside, of families watching evening television, and the general activity of private lives.

Here, in Edinburgh, we wanted to eagerly embrace all that we saw. We were like squeezed sponges, waiting to be put back in the water again, so that we could absorb everything.

Suddenly a loud 'oooh' at the rear of the coach had us all turning and craning. Fireworks were shooting high into the night sky, their coloured sprays in pink, blue and green; rockets exploding.

We turned a corner, waited at the lights, and I looked out to The Royal Mile, floodlit, its lights attached to the high buildings. It looked like a film set, waiting for the kings and princes of the past to arrive on horseback. Lost in my own dreams I gazed as we drove along the wide, straight thoroughfare, from the Palace of Holyroodhouse, past both old and new famous buildings, museums, the Scottish law courts, St Giles cathedral, ornate splendid libraries and ultimately, the narrower climb into Castle Hill, the route to

Edinburgh Castle. You can drive all the way. And it looked tonight as though Ted was going to do just that. I looked at my watch; 9.30pm.

Surely the Edinburgh Military Tattoo would be in full swing. That meant the castle would be out of bounds while thousands watched the spectacular show.

What did Ted have in mind? For most people on the coach this was a 'first outing' to Edinburgh. They were content to sit tight, enjoying every inch of the detour towards the castle.

Now we were just a few hundred metres away.

A kilted Highlander stepped out into the road with a police officer beside him. He raised his arm. Ted eased the coach to a halt, opened his window and started to talk.

The skirl of bagpipes and the loud roll of drums hit us. Necks craned to see more. And from a side street suddenly, amazingly, began to appear 'hundreds of thousands' of marching soldiers in full Highland dress: a huge military band of bagpipes, drums, trumpets, cymbals clashing and frontsmen twirling batons, their kilts swinging.

Like a crescendo the music flooded over us and filled to overflowing the narrow street sending it sky high to the 8th floor tenements above, where from open windows people leaned out waving small flags and cheering. Following the infantry pranced black horses carrying the mounted officers of the battalion and

17

Scots battle honours.

Suddenly we were part of it all, this giant show; the drum majors, tigerskins slung over one shoulder with bravado; foot soldiers in tartan trews with sparkling white spats over big black shiny boots. We watched in awe, our cameras snap-snapping, trying to catch the drama of this spectacle.

Proudly, defiantly, soldiers and horses turned and moved, as one, heading for the castle.

The rousing music that had echoed through the coach began to fade.

I wiped away a tear as beside me Don's cine film whirred.

It had taken a full five minutes for the marching army to go by. As they marched away up the hill to Edinburgh Castle, everyone in the coach started clapping and cheering and standing up to get a last view.

Ted was now deep in comfortable conversation with two Edinburgh policemen and the Highlander who had stopped him. It was all very affable. They were talking and laughing.

We were getting a front seat to this show. The Tattoo commentary was coming loud and clear over the sound system reverberating over the entire city.

'And now we have the massed bands of The Black Watch, just back from their tour of duty abroad' the voice boomed.

We listened as the audience sent up a tumultuous, wild cheer that went on and on. As The Black Watch marched on stage you could hear the bagpipes playing even louder and the drums rolling. We just sat, stunned.

Memories flooded back. I could remember nights when, cushion in hand and rug over my arm, I had often walked up this very street to be a part of the audience of a late night Tattoo. The cushion because the seats were hard wood and a rug to counter the cold of an Edinburgh night.

As the coach waited we were aware around us of people in various kinds of costume; young dancers in Highland dress, girls with white blouses and bodices of dark velvet. They too were now half walking and half dancing toward the esplanade.

Jill turned to me excitedly.

'Isn't this stunning? I had no idea.'

At that moment Dolly also found her voice. And turned to us.

'I'm overwhelmed. I just can't believe this is happening. It's exactly like a movie.' She sounded all choked up.

'I don't think we'll any of us sleep tonight' I said to both of them. 'It's as if the whole city is wide awake and celebrating.'

I heard Ted murmur a thank you and say cheerio. The coach started to edge very gently in reverse and to turn. The Highlander was behind the coach now and helping direct the manoeuvre. When a full turn was accomplished he crossed outstretched arms in farewell. And Ted toot-tooted on the horn. In the coach we looked back, cheered and waved and cheered again.

What an introduction to Edinburgh !!

Then Ted turned and said with a smile. 'I thought I'd give it a try. We had our own performance there.'

He seemed as happy as we all were.

Then he headed the coach forward turning left by Deacon Brodie's pub as the lights changed to green and we were going down The Mound.

Looking back we could see the lights and hear the cheers and applause of the Tattoo, high up from the castle, far above the city. Entranced we continued to watch and listen.

We turned into Princes Street, with its beautiful shops on one side and splendid gardens on the other. Within minutes we would be in Inverleith, just beyond Edinburgh's magnificent Georgian New Town.

Here we were, in the Scottish capital, tired but happy travellers.

We did not know it then but we were about to embark on the adventure of our lives.

# CHAPTER THREE

*A party at The Deerstalker*

Elated yet exhausted we stepped into The Deerstalker, our hotel for the next two nights.

We were late arriving. But the establishment, both grand and welcoming, with many deerheads decorating the entrance hall, was, it seemed, more than ready for us.

Ted was already organising the individual cases from the luggage compartment. And two young men were helpfully matching us up, cases to rooms.

Jill looked up at the large antlers. 'I see why it's called The Deerstalker' she said with a conspiratorial laugh.

'Yes. But it's nice, isn't it'

She agreed.

The oak panelled woodwork of the walls was finely carved and ornate heavy candelabras of Victorian design lit the room and beyond we could see what must have been the morning room with long deep blue floor to ceiling drapes.

There were paintings everywhere, from pictures of Edinburgh itself, to the typical Highland scene; lochs, mountains and glens, and toffee coloured long haired cattle, their horns looking quite devastating, but their faces soft and charming. I had to think the original fluffy toy must have been based on such a Highland creature.

Jill caught my gaze at the picture near to us.

'Different, aren't they?'

I nodded and smiled.

'I was thinking how lovely and almost unreal Highland cattle look.'

'I hope we see some.'

'We must ask Ted to make sure he goes the right way.'

At that we both laughed. He could manage most things and would probably know exactly where to find them. Our gaze swivelled to a dramatic sign in the foyer that seemed strangely, curiously, unwelcoming.

> 'WANTED. A reward of £ ¾ million is
> offered by the Police for the capture of
> thieves operating an International
> money laundering ring in Scotland.
> Tel: 0131 900 7643 with information.'

'That would be just like winning the lottery' I said to Jill, desperately trying to sound bright, little realising then that our holiday was about to change.

'Welcome drinks in the lounge' said a clear Scots voice behind us, distracting our thoughts.

A slim, dark haired woman in her fifties was smiling, waving us through.

It was Mrs Fiona McGill, the hotel proprietor, who introduced herself.

Leaving our cases in the hall we went towards a magnificent bar. There was every blend of whisky you can imagine and many that I had never heard of.

Even though whisky is not by any means my favourite drink, I was suitably impressed

'Holmes' now beside me - I really must start calling him by his real name, I thought - was looking astonished and delighted.

'This is most satisfactory' he said with a twinkle.

'I can see why Sir Arthur Conan Doyle liked it here.' He looked at me and smiled.

Within seconds two ladies behind the bar were pouring our drinks. And a small effusive party was in full swing.

Even Ted joined us, his labours done. He had 'parked up' the coach he informed us. Now here he was enjoying a whisky after a long, hard day's driving.

I reminded myself as I saw him in easy conversation with the American from Texas, tall, good humoured Don, that I really would ask him about Highland cattle. I bet he knows most of Scotland, I thought.

A voice beside me said suddenly 'Enjoying your dram?'

It was Heidi Oliver, at my elbow, smiling happily.

'Yes, I certainly am. What about you?'

She laughed delightedly. 'Yes and I am so pleased to be back in Edinburgh. It's been over twenty years.'

'..and for me too' I started to say.

We hadn't had the chance to chat before.

'Did you live here?' she asked.

'I most certainly did. Not more than twenty minutes walk away in the New Town.'

'I had a small flat off the Royal Mile' said Heidi. 'One of those elegant old fashioned 'closes'. I was working with a theatre company, the famous Traverse Theatre.'

'The tiny theatre that set the world alight' I said, remembering my forays there. 'Maybe I saw you in a play.'

We were just about to swap details when Mrs McGill started to speak. For a tiny lady, she had a very commanding voice as small ladies often do.

'We've arranged 'late supper' as you have missed the main evening meal. Edinburgh doesn't sleep when the Festival is on, you'll soon discover.'

She paused and we murmured our thanks. We certainly were hungry.

'All meet back here in twenty minutes. Time for you to see your rooms and splash your faces.'

Everyone laughed.

'We have a little 'entertainment' for you as well. Festival musicians and dancers are staying and they will be performing.' With that she was on her way. We looked at each other. Well, if this was Festival

Edinburgh, we were certainly in for a late, late night and a very good time.

'Shall we unpack?' I said to Jill, who was standing beside me now. She nodded and we each took our cases.

We found we had rooms on the second floor next to each other, which meant we would not get lost. And could easily rap on the others' door, to go downstairs.

For myself, unused to drinking whisky, the warming effect was making me feel quite relaxed and content. I dare not lay on my bed for I knew I should be fast asleep within seconds.

Instead I rummaged for my make-up, laid out my bed clothes and popped into the en-suite bathroom.

It was all very perfect; not too large, but large enough. White towels edged with blue borders and a white shower suite that sparkled caught my eye. It all looked inviting.

There were all those little niceties that women love, shampoos, shower cap, toothpaste and tiny, wrapped soaps and creams in sachets.

I brushed my hair, realising that it had been a long time since I had even looked at myself in the mirror.

I was looking slightly wan. A tap, tap on the door and Jill's voice calling out soon perked me up.

'Ready?'

I picked up my handbag 'Just coming.'

As I opened the door Jill peeped in.

'Oh lovely! Your room is blue and white, mine is soft coral and white. Aren't they splendid?'

'Yes' I enthused. 'I even have one of my Highland bulls on the wall.'

'You'll sleep well then.'

'Yes, when we finally get to bed' I laughed.

'I've often wondered if I live too quiet a life.' said Jill with a smile. 'Do you think they always celebrate so late in Edinburgh?'

'I think they are quite merry. It's a national habit, goes with the whisky.' I murmured, recalling the wild Edinburgh days of old. 'But this is Festival time, huge money spinner and also a big International audience and performers from just about everywhere.'

When I saw Heidi later she was keen to talk further. She had changed into a different top, in fashionable soft gold, a favourite evening colour this season. Her blouse was satin with a high cowl colour and long slim sleeves. It looked very good on her. She certainly knew how to wear the right clothes for every occasion.

Most other people, including Jill and myself, had not changed.

'I've a long list of friends who live in Edinburgh' said Heidi, interrupting my thoughts. 'Do you think I should give any of them a call tonight. It's a bit late, isn't it?'

I agreed that it was, adding 'I love your blouse. Very stunning.' I thought I should tell her. It was true.

'Oh, thank you.' She looked completely taken by surprise. 'I think I'll make my phone calls in the morning. It's ten-thirty already.'

We were walking towards the dining tables, pushed together to form one long table. This was more than a buffet. It was a sumptuous supper spread. And we were being invited to sit down.

Mrs McGill was standing nearby, talking to us, in a voice that made it imperative to listen. 'I usually like to have 'boy-girl, boy-girl' round the table. Ted's in the centre with a girl on either side.'

We all signalled our approval and at this Ted, who had just appeared from the hallway, went as pink as the shirt he had changed into. But with a broad smile he allowed himself to be led to his chair.

It worked out exactly like that; 'boy-girl' all round the beautifully decorated table, glasses shining, and table mats and silver cutlery as elegant as any that might grace dinner at the Ritz.

I finished up sitting between 'Holmes' on my right and an interesting young man in his mid thirties whom I had seen across the coach, but not yet spoken to; Charles Edward York. I discovered that he was Canadian and a lawyer. And his grandmother was a Stuart.

He was here hoping to do some research on Bonnie Prince Charlie, the Pretender to the Throne of Scotland, and he told me he had serious reason to believe that he was a great, great, great, great, great grandson of the Prince.

It began to make very real sense when he said that in his own family, every 'first son' for six generations had been given the names Charles Edward.

And that his forbears had settled on the East coast of Canada in 1790, the time of the Highland Clearances in Scotland, when thousands left for new lives in both America and Canada.

The failed Jacobite rebellion led by the young Stuart prince, alias Bonnie Prince Charlie, had indeed left many followers crossing the Atlantic by the thousand to seek a life in the new world.

My mind whirled. Could the handsome 24 year old Prince, when he fled to Rome and went into exile, have left behind a Scottish lass expecting his child? Was this young man a descendant of one of the illegitimate children of the Prince?

All this exciting background was in my head as I talked to this tall, brown haired young man, over my plate of delicious smoked salmon.

Charles Edward's Canadian drawl rolled easily of his tongue, yet his heart and his feelings were all right here in Scotland.

I had recently spent several weeks finding out all that I could about Bonnie Prince Charlie. It was amazingly coincidental.

But I thought I would keep that to myself for the

moment. After all I was here on holiday, trying to relax.
'Do you know Scotland well?' asked the Canadian.
'I lived here for fifteen years - in another life' I said
taking a sip of the white wine that had been poured
for me. He took the hint. And was not too curious. For
that I was grateful. 'I can probably give you a few leads
on your distant relative.'
He looked delighted. 'Well, thank you. That would be
splendid. I have some books with me.' He paused for
a moment. 'Of course I may be completely wrong about
this. We may not be related in any way.'
'But you are of Scottish blood.' I said quickly.
'Oh yes!' He sipped his drink too.
'Then you have every reason to think positively. And
as for the two forenames Charles Edward, that's
unusual.'
He brightened up. 'I guess it would make a good family
history novel if it were true.'
'It would be more than that. It would be like re-writing
history.'
I could feel that he too was excited by the idea. At that
moment the table began to be replenished with
Aberdeen Angus beef, dishes piled high with roast
potatoes, carrots, cauliflower and peas.
'I didn't think I was this hungry' I said helping myself.
He nodded. 'Nor me, but its very tasty. Scottish food
has a wonderful flavour.'

The noise of the party became deafening, as parties do when they are being enjoyed. I looked around. Everyone was talking, eating and drinking.

Mrs McGill was obviously a mistress at the art of hospitality. She knew the way to get us talking and making new friends.

Jill was happily, I could hear, chatting to 'Holmes' on her left. On her right was a white haired man, who later I was to discover, was a Scots born London GP, Dr Hamish Craig, from Greenwich, who was also travelling alone.

Heidi sat beside Don Oldenshaw and never stopped talking and laughing. The jollity flowed like wine as course followed course

I can't recall at what time the musicians and dancers arrived. But when they did we were all relaxed and merry. From a superb 'cello solo we were then treated to a small ensemble of musicians playing string instruments, and to fiddlers with lively dance music. Young dancers appeared, in Highland dress and performed, their kilts lifting to the swirl of their movements, and black ballet shoes pointing, as though toes were never intended to move in any other way.

Then followed the Highlander's sword dance. In full Highland dress with sgian dubh tucked into one knee-high sock, the young man leapt high in the air over crossed swords, dancing between them, expertly yet with ease. A bagpiper in full dress, piped as he danced,

We were all clapping and clapping in time to the music. Suddenly with a skirl of the pipes and a flourish it was over. The applause was deafening.

Minutes later as I made my way towards the lift and my room, I knew only that I would sleep well. And Jill, who was not far behind me, agreed.

What a night! We were exhilarated, tired and delighted all at the same time. And this was only day one of our Scottish holiday.

# CHAPTER FOUR

## *Some surprises*

I awakened to a cloudless blue sky and sunshine pouring in through the bedroom window. Outside a robin sang, its noisy chirrup, chirrup willing me to get up and get on with the day; telling me what a beautiful morning it was.

Then my alarm clock rang. Eight-thirty and my own particular 'dawn chorus' was in full swing.

I had thought I might have a slightly sore head. All that wine and whisky! Well, it seemed like lots of wine and whisky, to me. But when I stepped out of the folded quilted covers, tossing them back and getting onto my feet I realised that I felt absolutely terrific! I had slept dreamlessly and well.

Away in another room I could hear someone else's alarm clock ringing merrily. Then it stopped. Another sleepyhead awakening, I thought. And surmised it was probably one of our party, maybe Jill next door.

My phone rang just as I was stepping into the shower. It was beginning to sound like Piccadilly Circus at rush hour.

'Hi.' Jill almost leapt through the phone 'Sorry to bother you so early. Are you going down to breakfast?'
I said that I would be.
'Meet you in fifteen minutes on the landing.'
I stepped back and into the shower. And came out two minutes later, squeaky clean, ready to face whatever the day presented.
After so much travelling the sheer luxury of the bathroom; the whooshing of water like fountains from twin taps and being able to luxuriate in it all, was total bliss. It becomes more so as I get older.
I towelled dry. And began to dress choosing a light pale blue blouse and slacks in deep charcoal grey. The slacks, because, they trim me down a whole size making me look positively slender.
I turned sideways to look critically in the long mirror. And decided that I should not eat too much today. Last night was a feast, but I doubted if I would be able to lose the weight if we were going to eat so well every night. I had no desire to return to England two sizes larger from my foray North of the Border. The thought sent a shudder down my spine.
The Georgian window sash cords moved easily as I threw open the windows fully. The gardens below were alive with bright reds, blues and yellows; the flowers massed and verdant. It must have been a hot and sunny summer in Edinburgh too. Tall roses of every hue from amber to gold, soft pink and deep rich red,

spilled over a dour stone wall, at least two foot thick. We had had a lovely English summer. And I knew from my years in Edinburgh that their long hot summer days could often be almost as good.

When I opened the door Jill was on the landing talking to 'Holmes'

She looked lovely, in a lightweight oatmeal linen trouser suit, perfect for a day that was going to be hot. She turned to me full of excitement.

'Mr Watson was up early and looking up the history of this house. Guess what, it seems Sir Arthur Conan Doyle actually lived here. But not all the time.'

As we walked down the solid oak staircase, with its giant 1ft square carved corner pieces and red patterned carpet soft under our feet, we continued to dwell on the great writer who was born in Edinburgh. And took up writing after becoming a doctor.

John Watson was keen to interrupt with more news. He had a sparkling piece of information that even excited me, and I am not a true Sherlock Holmes fan.

'On August 28 1895 Conan Doyle was here dining late with a colleague, when he had the inspiration for one of his earliest mysteries. In those days this was the splendid residence of his good friend, Thomas McNaught.

'While they were dining they saw a strange character lurking in the roadway outside and then going into the house opposite. They became curious and decided to watch more closely.'

I was almost holding my breath. 'Then?'

'Well, the man was certainly up to no good. They took notes of his appearance and what he was about. Holmes - I mean Conan Doyle - actually left the dining room and followed the man into the garden of the house opposite. He saw him break a window and sneak in.'

'Didn't he do anything like, call the police?'

'Yes, it seems he did. The police arrived and by the time they did so, there was no sign of anyone. Neither did they notice that anything was stolen. No-one was there so that was the end of it.'

He smiled and continued. 'But they were wrong. The man was an unscrupulous lawyer, Scott McCree and he now had vital evidence for his client Horace Aventi, accused of the murder of a young woman, Rachael Donoghue. He was seeking paperwork, documents. And he found them all, on that night.'

'McCree was a clever and devious lawyer. The evidence he now had helped to free Aventi at the infamous Old Bailey trial in London early the next year.'

Jill, beside me, was incredulous.

Mr Watson looked elated.

As we neared the morning room I felt compelled to ask 'How do you know all this and so soon?'

'I was reading until the early hours of the morning after our little party. Another guest happened to tell me that last night was the exact date of the night that Conan Doyle had been here and seen the crime.'

'August 28.' Jill and I said it together and we looked at each other, amazed.

'Quite so.' Mr Watson laughed. 'When I told this Highlander that my name was Watson and I was a member of the Sherlock Holmes Society, he wanted to tell me everything and he produced a book about it all.'

'You had a brilliant time I'm sure, even though you must be exhausted.'

'Well, the exhaustion will, I fear, come later. For the moment I am still elated. Think what my colleagues at the Society will say.'

As we rounded the hall into the morning room, the scene of last night's partying, and this morning's breakfast, Jill said with a smile 'I've never been a Conan Doyle enthusiast but now that we are here with his work all around us, I think I could easily become one.'

'Something like this is all it takes. I started as a schoolboy, I admire the detective's sense of detail.'

Ted was already seated at a table close to the window. And as he seemed to be the first of our party, he looked over, grinned, and invited us to join him.

I could not resist referring to the 'wild night' before.

'Some people never did get to their beds, at least until dawn' he said laughing, and eagerly sipping a coffee that I noted was black and strong.

'Is that why there are so few down to breakfast? said Jill.

'Probably, but they'll get the smell of bacon and appear, I imagine, in the next twenty minutes or so.'

At that stage a waitress appeared, her red curls tied back with a bow and not more than 18 years of age.

'Coffee or tea?' she said and with her bright pretty smile went one-by-one around the table asking if we would like 'a full Scottish breakfast.'

We all said we would. And at that moment Ted's breakfast arrived to give us a hint of what was to come.

Eggs, bacon, mushrooms, sausage, black pudding, fried bread and tomato on an enormous plate filled to the very edge.

But, as Ted was to remind us, there was 'a starter'; orange or grapefruit juice, a choice of muesli, or Scots porridge oats, hot, served with cream in small white individual cream pots. I chose the porridge and found this satisfying and pleasing.

When it finally came to marmalade and toast I knew we were eating 'like lords' and I had quite forgotten any desire to diet! Then the red headed waitress appeared from the kitchen with a basket of piping hot scones - made that very morning. Irresistible...! We laughed and ate, and discussed the merits of Conan Doyle and between mouthfuls Mr Watson enlarged upon his overnight discoveries about the great writer.

Ted said he would take us along Leith Walk to see the

statue of Sherlock Holmes; a tribute to Sir Arthur Conan Doyle.

Ted was proving again to be an amiable driver and guide.

Other guests were drifting in for breakfast now and smiling  and saying their 'hellos', while I also touched upon the subject of our Canadian and his family research of Bonnie Prince Charlie.

'Bit like a history tour' said Ted, with an even bigger grin.

'I once took a whole coach full of Campbells on a tour of the Highlands to see Glen Coe.'  He saw our surprise and went on.  'It was mid-winter and we were caught in a snowdrift and had to get the emergency services  to hitch the coach out.'  He buttered another scone and spread it amply with marmalade.

'Glen Coe is very eerie even these days.  We were stuck there half the night.  People say the ghosts of the MacDonalds, murdered in their beds by the Campbells in 1692, still haunt the place today.'

He shuddered. 'It was chilling. I doubt if we will ever forget that night.'

'Did you get out all right?' said Jill.

'Just as the dawn came up over the mountains.  It was snowing and blowing half a gale, the sun came through and it all looked pink on the horizon but it was freezing. We were in boots, fur hats, wrapped in blankets and passing the whisky around, medicinal, to keep warm.'

He laughed, remembering. 'We headed for Aberdeen after that. At first no-one could stop talking about that night. Suddenly they were real Campbells. They seemed to be very close to their ancestors, then they became rather quiet as they realised the horror of it all.'

'Nothing like a trauma and the harshness to make it real' added Mr Watson, between mouthfuls of bacon.

I had to agree. 'Life is easy these days compared to then.'

'When we head somewhere like that I usually expect strange things to happen' added Ted thoughtfully.

'I've only ever had one trouble free run through Glen Coe and that was in high summer.'

'It's as if all the ghosts were reacting in some way' said Jill, who was now enjoying her breakfast.

'Yes, though no-one's ever analysed it. It just sends shivers down the spine.'

'Death' said Mr Watson, as though he was talking about a Sherlock Holmes mystery, rather than the demise of many at the Glen Coe massacre.

'Yes and on a terrible scale' added Ted, showing that he knew his Scottish history.

I wondered if he had always done the Scottish tours.

'For about ten years. I'm a bit like a walking history book' he smiled. Then screwing up his serviette and putting it on his plate, he rose. 'Right. I'm well set up for the day. They do a marvellous breakfast here - bit like a four course dinner. I'm off to check the coach.

See you in about an hour.'

With that he was off, passing a quick word with the porter in the foyer as he went and stopping for a word with one or two of the coach party, who were now settled and enjoying their large breakfasts.

Across the lovely, tranquil, room with its bouquets of dried roses and leaves plus gilt edged huge mirrors, looking very grand, and the walls in deep red silk wallpaper, voices of the breakfasters began to buzz.

A large white marble fireplace added to the elegance of the room; its bright and pretty ornaments on the marble shelf above.

In winter there would be a roaring fire but now polished brass accoutrements and a huge massed display of variegated summer flowers, pink and orange flecked lupins, bright blue and purple delphiniums, white daisies and roses decorated the space.

I suspected that a hint of their perfume would waft across the room later in the day when the stronger aromas of bacon and coffee had dispersed.

I noticed among the now crowded breakfast room, the happy and relaxed Texans, Don and his wife Dorothy Oldenshaw. They looked over and smiled warmly.

'I think I have had enough' said Jill, with a sigh, as though the final scone in the small basket on the table was still tempting her.

'What a wonderful breakfast' I said, swiftly agreeing, recalling my promise to myself not to eat too much.

The coach party was settling down in the most lively, amicable way. Mr Watson, busily reading his copy of The Daily Telegraph, said he would see us in a little while. He was savouring his coffee and wanted to look at the Holmes details one more time before we set off for the day's journey.

'Where are we off to, today?' I turned to ask Jill, but she was already ahead of me and talking to another coach party member.

'Ted said we may be going North'.

It was Dolly Whitby, the American whom I had hardly seen since arriving the night before. She looked relaxed and her face was, as ever, animated. Her American soft drawl I could have listened to all day.

'Hi Dolly. How are you this lovely morning?'

Smiling, she said 'I never thought they had any sunshine in Scotland. Now I know that all that talk of rain, rain, rain is not correct. The forecasters say it will be hot and sunny all week.'

'Wonderful' I sighed. 'It can rain here, and it snows - but not in August.'

'Do you think we shall go into your part of the world today?' I asked.

'You mean Rob Roy country?' She reached for a book. 'Look what I have here. Mrs McGill says I can borrow it while we are staying, so that I can read all about the man.' She smiled and pulled a face. 'But I fear he's not exactly a hero, is he, Rob Roy?'

'You mean you may not wish to have him 'in the family'?

She grinned broadly. 'I wouldn't go as far as that. I think it would be nice to know for sure. He was quite a rogue.'

'Do you think that Ted will let us choose where we go today?'

'There's so much to see, and lots of people on the coach are searching out their ancestors.'

Dolly was surprised. 'You mean Mr Watson?'

'No, he's a Sherlock Holmes fan. Mr Watson is finding out lots that is very interesting indeed about the writer of the famous detective stories. I was really thinking of Mr York. We think he may be related to Bonnie Prince Charlie, the young Pretender to the Throne.'

Her eyes widened. 'Really?'

I glanced across and could see the handsome Charles Edward York sipping coffee and reading at the same time. It looked as though he too had found a large historic book, and maybe was discovering more about his ancestors.

I pointed him out to Dolly. 'You two must have a chat.'

At that stage there was a general movement out of the morning room. I followed Jill and caught her up on the stairs.

'Did you know there was a break-in here last night?' she said curiously.

'No. Who said?'

'I've just been told by Don and Dorothy. They said that the police arrived at about 4am.'

I waited for her to continue.

'I gather that no-one was found. The hotel cameras picked up a man enterting and leaving by the back door.'

Recalling so vividly the man in armour who had stood at my bedroom door the night before, without thinking I said 'So we have a ghost as part of the coach party.'

Jill turned at the top of the stairs and looked amazed.

'That's exactly what Don said.'

I must have looked curious. On this hot, sunny morning ghosts seemed quite of place. Surely ghosts were for cold, foggy, frosty nights in November. And had anyone ever seen or heard of a ghost that went on a coach trip?

'Why did Don say that?'

'Well he thought that someone was sitting in the seat behind him all the way from Scarborough, where you saw your ghost. But when he asked Ted, it seemed the seat was empty.'

I waited for her to go on.

'He held a conversation with this guy when we were driving into Edinburgh during all that rain last night and the man kept asking questions. Don was absolutely certain he was real'.

'Did he see him?'

'No, but he says he tapped him on the arm and then they

started talking. Of course it was quite dark in the coach anyway.'

Should I have shivered? I don't know. I just felt a slight chill as I turned to enter my bedroom. We had so many people trying to trace their ancestors, had one of their ghosts from the past joined the party?

Was it the kind of thing I could ask Ted, without getting him worried? I decided to delay this for a day or so.

Let's just see what happens today, I thought with a half smile. Maybe the ghost of Bonnie Prince Charlie is with us. Or perhaps Sherlock Holmes was playing tricks and it was all Mr Watson's doing.

I said to Jill that I would knock on her door before going downstairs. We had been told to be back in the morning room at 9.45am, where Ted would meet us and we could decide our plans for the day.

I switched on the radio and heard BBC Scotland, with all the local news. The lilt of Scottish voices and the local place names, made me relax. Now I was truly here in Scotland.

When we assembled Ted did his usual passenger count. This time he had a clipboard and looked rather official. When I asked him why, he said that once they had left someone behind. He grimaced as he said it, not liking to remember the trouble it had caused.

We all felt slightly like schoolchildren; happy schoolchildren. We were off for a day in the Highlands, it had been decided. And would be back staying at The

Deerstalker again tonight.

After going through the list Ted stepped aside. And then returned. 'Has anyone seen Heidi this morning?'

We all looked at each other, blankly.

'I'll check her room' said the porter, and vanished.

Two minutes later he was back, with a face that could not conceal his feelings. It was the most open face I'd ever seen, rather like a small boy's.

'She's not there, she's gone'.

Ted looked at the man. 'What d'you mean, gone..?'

He handed Ted a note which he quickly read. The look of relief on his face was followed by a short 'Oh'.

Everyone waited for a response. After all she was part of the coach tour. We felt involved.

'She's all right' he said, slightly sheepishly, I thought.

'One of the Highlanders here last night was someone she knew. Heidi says she'll see us next week.'

There was a slight gasp, or more, an indrawn breath. No-one was even mildly shocked. But everyone had a sense of slight surprise and then, 'Well, why not?'

Heidi was out to enjoy her holiday. Good on her!

We wondered which Highlander. No-one could work that out.

Ten minutes later, the coach party, which we had now decided to label 'The Bonnie Prince Charlie Tour' partly because it sounded rather exciting, was heading for South Queensferry, where we would see the Forth Railway Bridge, the eighth wonder of the world!

We would cross the Firth of Forth by the road bridge, providing a superb view of it all. Don, with his camera and cine at the ready, would, I knew, be in his element.

'I hope you *are* related to the Bonnie Prince' I said to Charles Edward who was now sitting beside me.

'Me too' he said with a broad smile, his eyes sparkling. 'He was quite a charismatic sort of guy'.

Then his mobile phone rang. He was being called from Toronto.

'Guess what, it may be true' he said into the small hand phone. 'We're heading for the Highlands right now'.

I snuggled down into the softness of the coach seat. And smiled. What a crazy trip this was turning out to be. And all because of the amazing people on it. Everyone was here, it seemed, for a different reason.

As for me I had merely been hoping for a brief respite from the South Coast and a chance to recapture some of the charm and beauty of Scotland's glens and mountains and sparkling rivers. They enchanted me and refreshed my spirits whenever I saw them again.

# CHAPTER FIVE

## *A Highland glance*

We were north of Stirling castle, standing proud and high  guarding its famous city  to its heart when I saw my first  Highland cow, not just one, but at least a dozen. Their toffee-coloured long hair covered beautiful round eyes that peeped out from rumpled brows.

Long, dangerous looking horns belied cuddly,  warm placid faces and their coats  seemed  more like those of fluffy toys.  I found my camera and snap-snapped.  And could hear others in the coach doing likewise.

Ted had to stop  on the narrow road, at a passing point, which gave us ample time. We were well rewarded.

He  had already told us that part of the fun of this trip was going to be  'making new friends'. His  plan was that no-one should stick to  'the same seat' and 'the same neighbour' all  the time. So it became a game we played. Every time we stopped for coffee, lunch - or just to enjoy a special view - we switched seats: it was a bit like musical chairs!

Charles  had  now  moved  and  was  sitting  quietly explaining his Bonnie Prince Charlie theories to Jill in the seat in front, while I   sat next to Dorothy Oldenshaw. Apart from occasional hellos we had hardly had time  to speak previously.  Now  she was telling me about their   ranch back home in the US; their own cattle, rather different than the Scottish variety, but just as 'adorable', a word that she used and it slipped off her tongue in a broad  Texan accent, easily. We liked each other immediately.

She was a small, wiry,  woman in her forties, dressed neatly always, in slacks, usually beige or tan, with a short-sleeved blouse.  Like all Americans she had a wonderful sun tan, the kind that you felt never left her. You could tell she was a farmer's wife and  that she knew her cattle. She talked expertly but without fuss about their own breeds back home. She liked to hand rear her  young calves.

Husband  Don was  tough, wiry and like a  string bean. This was the first holiday they had had in twenty years, and their first ever time back  to her  homeland, Scotland.

Homeland?  Well, that was how  she phrased it. Then she explained. Her grandmother had emigrated from Dunoon.  And they just knew that on her side everyone was a Scot. Her family name was Robertson.

'And is Don a Scot too?' I asked.

'No, he's pure European, Greek  grandparents' she said with a laugh, adding  'What a mixture we are. But we are workers. Most farmers in Texas are.    It's tough.

We just get on and do things. Mind you I love being back here in Scotland. I think I get my workaholic tendencies from my Scottish grannie.'

She wanted to know all about me.

I told her that I had lived in Scotland for fifteen years. And married a Scot and that I too, had a Scottish grannie, from Wick, which is the far, far North of Scotland, adding 'When I arrived here as a young woman I felt immediately 'at home'. It was so strange because I was born in London.'

'The ancestry, your Scottish grannie' laughed Dorothy, understanding immediately.

'Yes, but at the time, I remember, I wondered how it could be. I even had difficulty understanding the language.'

She listened intently as I continued.

'I discovered, quite by chance, my grandmother's Scottish history. Then it all suddenly slotted into place.'

She sighed. 'I feel strongly about my Scots origins too. We've traced back some of our family.'

'And are you visiting them while you are here?'

'Yes, we hope to. We were on the phone last night trying to set up a meeting next week. They are either going to travel to see us in Edinburgh one afternoon or the plan is we will go over to Glasgow.' She smiled broadly. 'That's been another of my lifelong ambitions, all my life, to see Glasgow.'

'All that history and building great iron ships that sailed the seas, often to America' I added, feeling nostalgic too.

'I believe it's as exciting as Edinburgh but very different.'

'Yes, a wonderful city. Full of liveliness, and humour and culture too. I love it equally' I said, recalling Sauchiehall Street and the huge fashion shops, the broad, hilly, busy streets that always remind me of San Francisco.

'I think you'll love it there.' I said. 'We'll have to get Ted taking some detours.'

She laughed. 'We've already asked and he seems game to go on a roundabout tour, so long as everyone agrees.'

'That's fabulous.' I said. How enterprising of an American that she should already have asked Ted and got his virtual OK. She was a business woman through and through. Doing things for herself, rather than waiting for someone else to set them up for her. She and her husband Don seemed to have the closest bonds, but were still very individual. They were already happily making friends and sharing their own quite different lives with us.

Who is looking after the ranch back home, I asked?

'Our sons Rod and Travers. They're married with young families. They insisted that we should come on this trip.' she smiled happily, her eyes lighting up.

'I think they felt we should  research the family history and they  wanted to  prove they could run the ranch successfully.'

'I'm sure they can.' I said

She looked very proud. 'They're  pretty good.'

Across the aisle  John Watson was expounding a theory about Sherlock Holmes, much to the serious interest of Dolly Whitby.   He had a reference book on his knee and they were deep in conversation.

I thought how unusual it all was. It would have been unlikely such a couple could have met and got to know each other in normal circumstances.

John Watson, a retired Metropolitan police inspector, was a man who had made the London police his whole life. Now,  retired,  he  was  still  working  as  an investigator  with his fictional hero.  He seemed in his element.

I wondered, with a smile, whether as  the tour progressed, we would have a need for such obvious expertise.  We may well.

We had a doctor on board, Edinburgh-born, Dr Hamish Craig;  a mechanic and 'second driver' in the shape of Harry Sparrow, the chirpy London  bus  driver;  Jill, a school teacher;  Dorothy and Don,  ranchers  from Texas; a Canadian lawyer,  Charles Edward York and Dolly, I paused and  wondered what her career had been. Heidi, the dancer, I felt sure we would see before the tour  was  through  and we had others that I had not yet really spoken to. Many of us were here on our own missions trying to work out our own complex family histories. I was hoping to find more traces of my Scottish great grandmother, the illustrious Pheobe; mother of ten; five girls and five boys, who all survived and became part of London's academic culture in the late 1800's.

We were a diverse and lively party with backgrounds from just about everywhere in the world. We had two Singaporean girl students on the coach who smiled and said little; but, I gathered, were hoping to improve their English plus a handsome dark haired, olive skinned Mediterranean, who looked neither French nor Italian and I later discovered was from Marseille.

We would all get to know each other in time, I thought. Ted would see to that.

A mobile was ringing in the coach. And Dolly stopped talking to John Watson to answer it.

Two seconds later, delighted and amazed, she said out loud. 'It's New York!'

Later Dolly told me it was from her sister Madge, with whom these days she shared a New York apartment. They had had a plan to 'try out' the mobile phone just to see if it would reach Scotland. Neither had thought it really would.

Both she and Mr Watson it seems, were having the most enlightened historical conversation when the phone rang. He had delved into a book that told her lots more about the MacGregors and the infamous Rob Roy, a cattle thief and robber if ever there was one. She looked suitably impressed.

'I really don't know whether he's an antecedent or not' she laughed, her blue eyes twinkling. 'I haven't told my sister anything yet.' She thought for a moment. 'I'll find out a little more, if I can, and then decide if we should disown him or not.'

'That's a very sound idea' I said, realising that it would be one thing knowing you had a famous name in the family but quite another if he or she was a rogue.

'Mind you he is fantastically famous.' I added 'Sir Walter Scott, the great novelist, wrote Rob Roy, a hugely successful and romantic book about the man. And recently it was turned into a tremendous film starring Liam Neeson.'

Dolly looked impressed and I could see was clearly re-thinking her rash earlier deliberation.

'I'll try to get a copy of the book while I'm here' she said happily.

We were heading along between open fields with sparkling rivers that took my breath away on this sunny end of summer day. Also, it was becoming quieter - or was that an illusion? I would ask Ted later. Was there always less traffic in Scotland? It certainly seemed so.

Beyond Stirling the terrain was beginning to change. We were steadily rising, the road curving and turning

with hills ahead in the distance as far as the eye could
see. It was as if the whole world was opening out
before our eyes.

Suddenly as we turned a sharp corner a sheep stood
blocking the road. It bleated. And had no thought to
move. Ted brought the coach to a halt, changing gear
with a grind. When we looked up we saw a lone piper
in full Highland dress standing at the roadside playing
the bagpipes to an audience of sheep, hills and sky.

Almost as one we reached for our cameras and snapped
excitedly.

Ted drew the coach into a lay-by at the side of the
road. And as though by mutual consent we all trooped
out to feel the cool breezes and breathe in this vast
expanse of beauty and air.

Jill, ahead of me, ran back to get a cardigan.

'It's windy up here' she said, her voice being thrown
into the wind and away toward the mountains.

Ted said nothing but looked about. You could see that
he loved the view too. He just sat down on a knoll of
earth and looked and looked. The piper went on piping.

~ ~

When we returned to The Deerstalker much later we
were in for an amazing and mysterious night: one that
was tailor made for our sleuth, John Watson.

It set the tone for the rest of the tour. We quickly

realised that anything could happen.

Within days every newspaper and television company would be on the hotel's doorstep, all seeking an 'eye witness' quote.

I guess hotels don't usually announce when a celebrity arrives. People just 'notice' the familiar face, maybe from stage or screen, in the foyer. And the word spreads. Though with so many TV faces these days they crop up everywhere. But this was different.

The star was Hollywood! And her movie - a Scottish film - was being premiered in Edinburgh this week as part of the Festival.

Jill mentioned it first at our evening meal.

'Have you seen the girl with the fabulous red hair? The film star.'

I said I hadn't. We were busy enjoying the most delicious soup, Scotch broth, a light soup, based on shoulder of mutton, with chopped leeks and carrots and pearl barley. Quite superb.

John Watson joined us, after asking if he might, apologising for being fifteen minutes late.

'Don't worry. I think most people are late, what an incredible day' I enthused. 'I fell fast asleep for an hour. All that fresh air. Jill wakened me.'

He laughed. I thought how much our 'Holmes' was changing. He was now almost extrovert. I really liked him. And he obviously enjoyed our company. He was always smartly dressed and now no longer wore his cape but a casual jacket and slacks. He was an enthusiastic traveller. Jill asked him about the film star. He had not seen her. But seemed interested.

Just then there was a noise in the foyer and we caught a glimpse of the star. She was surrounded by people and yet, for a moment, stood alone, and even popped her head through the open door. She gave us the most beautiful happy smile. Her face radiant and red hair glistening.

She seemed to be looking for someone, or at least hoping to see someone, then she turned away, waving her slim, pretty hand and wiggling her fingers, to acknowledge us. It was almost a child-like movement. And we were all immediately entranced.

Gloria Franklin wore a long royal blue, slimly cut evening gown that curved and swathed around her slender figure and fanned out into a fish tail below the knee. I caught a glimmer of a strappy silver sandal at her feet and a glittering necklace and then the image was gone, in an instant.

'That was nice' I said. 'Now we have seen the famous star.'

Both Jill and John murmured in agreement.

'Lovely girl.' said Jill.

John, busily buttering a brown roll, while he awaited his soup, added his own compliments. 'Stunning. She looks part Scottish; the red hair.'

We settled down to continue the most delicious meal;

poached fresh Scottish salmon, with small potatoes and an array of superb freshly cooked vegetables. Outside we were aware of cameras flashing and movement in the foyer, then suddenly it was all quiet. Our film star had left for her premiere.

When we finished eating it was time for coffee and liqueurs, Drambuie of course, a true Highland drink of utter perfection.

This whisky based liqueur is still created to a closely guarded recipe of the Mackinnon family, handed down through the centuries by word of mouth from the man we were now on our way to research; Bonnie Prince Charlie!

I sipped my liqueur carefully. Drambuie is pure nectar; smooth and rich, with an edge that leaves the flavour still on the tongue long after it has vanished from the mouth.

All three of us agreed it was, without doubt, the most perfect after dinner drink. It hardly needed the fine dark chocolate mints that we were also enjoying.

'I'm going to go straight back to sleep again' I said, laughing. 'I feel pleasantly mellow and totally exhausted.'

'Great, isn't it' said Jill 'This is why I come to Scotland on holiday, to 'wind down'.

John was already deep into other thoughts. And said he was wondering where we would be going tomorrow.

Ted appeared through the door and walked over. He

seemed surprised that we were the only ones in the dining room. 'Where's everyone?' he inquired looking worried. 'Think I'll get reception to give them a call.'

But at that moment through the door stepped a whole party from the coach. They were full of apologies adding that they too had fallen sound asleep.

Ted told us all about the evening's entertainment that was planned: a ceilidh; a Scottish evening of music, dance and drinks; a party! It would start in the lounge following dinner.

I exchanged glances with Jill, meaning that though I would love to take part, it seemed most unlikely. I was far too relaxed to consider dancing and more drinks. At ten o'clock I said my farewells and quietly climbed the stairs for bed. No rocking tonight. I knew I would sleep like a log.

Yet that's not quite what happened. I awakened at 2am, switched on my bedside light and listened. What had disturbed me?

The hotel was not quite quiet. But then some people, just home from the Festival clubs and parties, would not yet be in bed.

There were voices in the corridor; voices I did not know.

A man's voice said. 'Ah... but which room?'

I remembered that and later told the police. Why did I remember it word for word? And so clearly.

It seemed such a simple, yet incomplete thing to say.

Did anyone reply to the question?

'No' I said to the police. 'No, they didn't and I must have fallen asleep after that. But I'd know the voice, anywhere!'

That statement was due to haunt me. Why did I even say it? Something in my psyche had been stirred, it was true. I would know the voice when, and if, I heard it again.

In the morning the hotel was agog with people, many of them police in plain clothes. I peeped out of my room and then decided to ring Jill next door.

'What's going on?'

'I believe there was another intruder last night.' She sounded quite alarmed.

'You're joking.'

'No. It's serious. John Watson says that the hotel has strange things happening. Or else that there is a ghost'

'Shall we go down for breakfast ?' I said quickly.

John was already in the morning room, sipping black coffee. He smiled and half stood inviting both Jill and I to join him.

'The coffee is superb.' He reached for two extra cups.

I half hoped that he would talk about the events of the night. But he did not.

Outside it was a fine sunny morning; the windows were slightly raised and the birds were singing. It promised to be another lovely day. Yet we were worried.

'I think the great detective  is here right in the very fabric' said John 'They have all the letters and papers of Holmes,  even his unsolved cases. Someone here is a true enthusiast,  a collector.'

'Why don't you ask?' I said suddenly.

Having poured our coffees John continued.

'I have. I  spoke to  Mrs McGill last night when I saw her in the hall.   She said that a year ago I could have seen all  the  papers,  but  not  now  because  of  what happened. She seemed quite upset.'

Now Jill and I were listening hard. He  had our total concentration.

We waited for him to say more.  But he didn't.

'Well..?' said Jill, eventually.

'I asked Ted about it  and he said that he had heard that Mrs   McGill's   husband   had   died   in   strange circumstances.'

'He  said I was  not to dwell on it too much.   It's just that it seems  she was finding it hard to cope and had very nearly sold up.'

'That's sad.'  I was  sipping my coffee. Luckily it was black  and  strong.   I  needed  it  to  help  my  slightly shattered nerves.

'Not murder?'  said Jill.

'Why did you say  that?' asked John.

'I don't know. It was like an unbidden thought. It just came out.' She looked slightly alarmed.

Through the windows I could see  the  sun and hear the

breeze against the leaves on the trees.    It seemed too lovely a day for such  thoughts. Outside all  was serene and beautiful.

'Tell me about last night' said John  suddenly turning to me.

'You've heard then?'

He nodded. And said nothing.

'About 2am  I heard a man's voice in the corridor. He was asking for a room'

'Which room?'

'I fell asleep, that's all I heard.   I was so exhausted. It's not much help I'm afraid.'

'You know some priceless  jewellery   was stolen?'

'No  one was hurt. They  got away' said John, adding, thoughtfully. 'Better put any valuable jewellery into the hotel safe tonight'

Jill and I looked at each other. Neither of us wore any diamonds and said so.

John went back to sipping his coffee.

And then we moved over to a spare table to have breakfast, our appetites slightly diminished.

Ted wandered over and said that  following breakfast a police officer would be chatting to us, informally, about last night.

He added that it would not hold us up much.

Everyone was talking about the overnight  robbery.

But Charles Edward was also keen to know when and where he could research his family history.

'Here in Edinburgh, Register House and the Royal Scottish Museum. They're both handy. I'll point them out as we pass' said Ted, helpful as ever.

And Dolly wanted to walk the length of The Royal Mile.

'OK' said Ted. 'We'll do that too, but can we make it tomorrow?'

Dolly smiled and agreed.

The young policeman arrived as we moved into the foyer and said he was sorry to hold us up. He repeated that we should make sure we left no valuables in the hotel and that special instructions would be left in our rooms for later.

He was pretty upbeat and not at all 'a Sherlock Holmes' as John was to remark later.

'Enjoy your holiday. We're here to make sure you are looked after' added the police officer.

Jill looked at me and smiled as if to say, well, thank goodness for that.

'Can you tell us what was stolen?' asked John suddenly.

The officer hesitated for a moment and then said 'I don't see why not. You'll read it in the papers later. It was the diamond and sapphire necklace and earrings worn by Gloria Franklin last night, worth about £250,000, we're told.'

There was a general gasp of surprise.

'No one was hurt. We may ask a few questions later.

But that's all for now.' He turned to Ted, who was at his side and wondering if we could now go.

Ted looked at us and then at his watch. 'See you back here in fifteen minutes. We're off to the Borders today.'

Suddenly everyone rushed to get away.

On the coach Ted had one further announcement to make. The two Singaporean girls had packed and left the hotel. No sign of them.

When the coach party collectively gasped, he said 'It's not unusual. Often foreign youngsters see somewhere they like and decide to continue on their own.'

At that he switched the radio on to hear a lively dance track and whirled the coach in the general direction of Dalkeith, South of Edinburgh.

We were heading for Scott country, Sir Walter Scott country. And I was rather pleased that soon we would be in the lovely countryside of the Scottish Borders and away from the machinations of whatever was happening at The Deerstalker.

# CHAPTER SIX

## *The Devil's Beef Tub*

Ted drove out of Edinburgh, almost, it seemed to me, as fast as he could. It had been a worrying night. And with many unresolved problems.

Who had taken the jewels at The Deerstalker? Would they return again tonight?

And where were Lin and Myleen, the two girls from Singapore? They had added a delightful touch to the coach party. And were always happy and smiling and seemed to be thoroughly enjoying the whole atmosphere of the tour. Now we were about to embark upon the most interesting part it seemed strange that they had left, without even leaving a note.

John was sitting just alongside me, across the aisle and leaned forward as the coach buzzed through the narrow tenemented streets of the 'old town' and we headed for Dalkeith.

He was looking thoughtful as he turned to talk.

'You know how The Deerstalker got it name?'

I was still not thinking straight but musing on the look of the weather for the day: suddenly it seemed to be clouding over. And other thoughts were troubling me still; like the film star and the missing jewels. It was all very strange.

But John continued. 'Holmes's deerstalker hat. It was his 'logo', that and his cape and the magnifying glass.'

'Yes I guess it was.'

John had a book in his hand, one that he had borrowed from another member of the coach party.

'I believe this was not so much his good friend's house, as Mrs McGill has said, but his own house. Maybe even just leased, but definitely his.'

John was getting quite 'into it' And I listened intently. Though I am not a Sherlock Holmes reader, I could see what fascination it would hold for him. And for many others.

John had already said he was on the tour specifically to find out more about his illustrious 'hero'. Now he was finding it all, quite by chance, falling neatly, into his lap.

'It's all very possible' I said.

'Mrs McGill said she has some papers. These could be the missing works of Conan Doyle.' Now he sounded quite jublilant.

'There's something here' John flicked through his travel paperback and pointed to a reference. Then started to read aloud, but very quietly.

'At least two of Conan Doyle's later works have never been found. 'The Case of the Mysterious Monster' and

'Dr Watson Returns'.    The second book - about Watson - Conan  Doyle decided never to publish because  it would have made his assistant far too important in his own right.'

'It was at about this stage that, tired of Sherlock Holmes, Conan Doyle decided to  'kill Holmes off'. This caused a huge public outcry. By then people thought that Holmes was  a real detective   not just   a fictional character.'

John paused for a moment. 'Like to hear more?'

I nodded.

Why not?   I was learning all about  Sherlock Holmes the fast way. And I was fascinated.

He continued, having turned the page.

'One of the missing stories is set in the Highlands. Conan Doyle  spent a  summer researching and  writing the book and then agonised about publishing it.  It was 'The Case  of the Mysterious Monster.'

'It was rumoured   to be among his private possessions following his death  A  family member knew where it was but kept quiet as a promise to Conan Doyle. Maybe it awaits discovery by  an intrepid Holmes fan.'

John continued reading aloud.

'But where  to look?  Edinburgh salerooms and auction houses. Conan Doyle was born in Edinburgh in 1859 and  graduated from Edinburgh University as a bachelor  of medicine in 1881. He had both family and friends all his life in Edinburgh.'

'He lived in    Plymouth on the South coast of England where he first   went into practice as a young doctor, then moved to    Southsea,  near Portsmouth, where he had a   medical   practice.   Study In Scarlet, his    first Sherlock Holmes story, was published  in 1887. Conan Doyle was 28 years of age, an ambitious writer and a very hard-up doctor.'

John suddenly stopped and   looked up. 'Sorry,   I'm boring you.  I could go on and on.'

But I was  listening with keen interest.

'The Case of the Mysterious Monster.' I smiled   and said 'That could be the Loch Ness Monster.'

John nodded.  'Loch  Ness   in the Highlands   was a great favourite of all authors at the time.  That would account for Conan Doyle deciding not to publish.    It might have been considered too frivolous.

'People were taking Holmes very seriously.  They wrote asking him to solve their crimes.  For him to start writing about a sea monster  would have been  to say the least, a little bizarre  and  even perhaps  the subject of ridicule.'

My eyes must have widened. John continued with enthusiasm.

'Are we going anywhere near   Loch Ness?'

'We'll  ask Ted.'

At that we both laughed.

Jill looked across and smiled. 'You two look as though you have won the lottery.'

'Maybe we have' said John with a bright, inquisitive eye.

But we were very serious. We would ask Ted if we could go by way of Loch Ness. I felt sure he would agree.

The coach was now speeding beyond Dalkeith and along the A701. There was little traffic. The sky overhead was part blue and part cloud

John lapsed into contemplative silence.

I was glad that I had thought to pop a raincoat over my arm before leaving.

Everyone on the coach was pretty quiet today, I thought. Dolly, in the seat directly in front of me, turned round and smiled broadly. 'Ted told me he is heading first today for something that might interest me. It's a huge natural fold in the hills, called, I believe The Devil's Beef Tub. Gosh, that's an amazing name.' Her voice drawled beautifully; laconically.

She was holding a map in her hand. 'I wonder if you can locate it here for me?'

I said I would try. I knew vaguely that it was quite near Moffat. I had only ever come across it once, and by chance, in the old days. But I had never forgotten it for its sheer size and drama.

'Here.' I pointed to it on the map and handed the guide back to her.

'Ah' she smiled. 'Thank you. Why is it so important?'

'Cattle rustlers in the old days. It's a natural deep, fold

in the hills and was perfect for hiding cattle and sheep by the thousand. They said you could put 10,000 cattle there and not one be seen for months on end. That was in the days when cattle rustling was big business.'

'Don't ask me how the word 'devil' became part of the name. You'll have to be imaginative about that.'

'People like Rob Roy?' Dolly queried.

'Possibly. Did you tell Ted that you were a MacGregor?'

'Yes, last night at dinner. He said that when we go North in a couple of days we should be able to visit Rob Roy's grave at Balquhidder. And there's a very good museum too. It was then that he thought we might all like to see this amazing Border scenery today.'

'Are you researching your clan history while you are here?'

'Well, no, not really. I grabbed a couple of family details before I left home. I just wanted to see how I felt about Scotland, after all it is my ancestral 'homeland'.

I smiled and nodded.

'And what do you think so far?'

Her eyes lit up and sparkled 'I just love it.'

I was listening and thinking. This is what so many people feel whose ancestors come from this land of such strong contrasts and turbulent history. Deprivation sent thousands of Scots to Canada and the Americas, in the 1790's and onwards. They made a new and exuberant life.

Now here were their descendants, trooping back, not quite sure why they had such strong homeland feelings but wanting to see and feel their ancestral roots.

They were proud to be linked and carrying on Scotland's traditions in these faraway, and quite different, lands.

I mused upon it quietly. And the coach trundled on. We were now into beautiful open countryside. Sheep on the low rolling hills and trees stretching into the distance. The views were open and you could see for mile after mile after mile.

I could hear Dolly, flicking through the guide book on her lap. Then she handed round the side of the seat a bag of sweets for me to take one, and offered one to John also.

Once again the coach settled into cosy silence. Except for the quiet sound of the engine, little could be heard but a few whispered voices at the rear.

Ten minutes later the countryside seemed even more open and almost wild. There were fewer trees and we were climbing.

We turned a long bend in the road and suddenly Ted's microphone crackled into life.

'Look to your left and you'll start to see the beginning of the Devil's Beef Tub. I'll pull in to a lay-by in a moment and we can get out for a closer look.'

There were gasps from all sides as, suddenly, craning heads peered towards the deep, deep delve in the rolling hills. From the coach it seemed bottomless. And it is.

Yet I knew that soon we would be looking at it with no windows in between and then the real delight - and amazement - would swing into place. Some would even feel, as I had, a sense of vertigo.

It was vast and awesome. I wondered how the rest of the coach party would view this natural phenomenon in the high secluded hills of the Border country.

We were all piling out of the warm coach.

It was windy and the very first thing that happened was that one of the party lost his hat. It whisked up into the sky and sailed over and over and far away towards the Devil's Beef Tub.

Quickly Ted shouted out; his voice swept away by the gusts. 'Don't go after it Mr Jenkins. I've seen bad accidents that way. We'll either pick it up later, or we won't be able to.'

Mr Jenkins, a gentleman who had so far kept quite a low profile, looked slightly alarmed but took Ted's advice.

We all watched as the check cap twirled and twirled, nearly came down, and then whisked far, far away over the hills, as though it intended never to settle or come to earth. I could see it would be miles away, far beyond the verdant gorge in the hills. And who would find it then? Maybe a passing rook or crow looking for fabric, attracted by the colour, building its nest.

I shivered slightly and then wondered why. It was only a cap. Yet it sent a chill through me. John was standing close by. And we smiled.

'I hope you have your hat well pulled on.'

He grinned and nodded.

'It's very deep. I'm petrified' I said turning to Dolly who was busy taking pictures.

'Do be careful. What do you think of it?'

'I can see why it got the name 'devil'. It's pretty frightening. It's so vast.'

The Oldenshaws were busy whirring with their cine camera.

And just then I heard Ted say 'Don't anyone please try to venture down. We've had accidents here in the past. Be careful.'

Around us the wind whirled and whistled; it began to rain and as I looked back towards this huge enclave in the hills, it seemed more like a cauldron than a beef tub. It was spooky, even in broad daylight. And it was suddenly so windy that you felt you were, with the next gust, likely to the thrown in to the very depths.

I could sense that Ted was anxious, nervous; eager to get his flock back into the warm safety of the coach. By now we were all shivering.

John half shouted suddenly 'Ready?'

I nodded and with Dolly and Jill joined him to walk

back. And the whole party keeping together, we pushed against the wind to reach the coach entrance.

'Bit lonely here at night' said John.

'Yes, it reeks of plunder, don't you think. Almost as though its dark history lives on.'

He agreed.

Mr Jenkins, hatless now, stepped back into the coach and went to his seat.

'Sorry about that' said Ted. 'I hope you've another hat with you.'

'Yes, I have' he said with a chirpy smile, pulling one immediately from his pocket. 'Think I'll tie it on.'

Everyone laughed gently.

Ted counted us all, like precious sheep.

How awful to be left here, I mused. But kept that to myself. It was lonely, on this road. We had seen, while being here, no other car or van or lorry. Or bicycle.

Soon we were moving again; the coach engine a comfort to our ears and our senses.

'Well, did you like that?' asked Ted breezily from his driving seat.

There was a general buzz of conversation all around as everyone settled down.

Suddenly a female voice from the back said. 'The Beef Tub made me feel as small as an ant.'

There was a murmur as though everyone agreed.

Dolly turned to me 'I wonder if Rob Roy was ever here?'

'I think so' I said with a half smile.

The coach was moving  down, down, back towards civilisation again. Around us the hills suddenly had trees and there  were side roads as the countryside became  more populated with small houses and farms.

Ted was going to take us through a Border town and I hoped we would stop for coffee.

Maybe there would be delectable scones of the sort that only Scotland can boast; the huge variety  and scrumptious flavour enticing and unique.   I could hardly wait !

~ ~

Later at The Deerstalker we  retraced our steps of the day over a dinner of fine venison. And we talked and laughed the night away.

It was Ted's  44th birthday and Mrs McGill had learned this and decided to surprise him and all of us with a birthday banquet.

From happy birthday sung at least three  times and even a splendid iced birthday cake, there were also crazy games to be played. And fiddlers to dance to.

The young police officer looked in to say that we had no cause to be alarmed about the events of the previous night; they would be on duty at the hotel all night.

The evening ended with a Highland reel, which we were all taught.

By popular agreement the day in the Borders that had taken in a stately home, a castle and Melrose Abbey plus a wonderful Scottish village bakery that served us hot scones: treacle, cinnamon, sultana, malt and even whisky scones, with lashings of butter, was an amazing adventure.

Tomorrow we would be heading for the Highlands, the glens and mountains. And would be away for two days. I slept like a lamb and awoke early, unable to contain my excitement.

*The Rob Roy and Trossachs Visitor Centre is at Ancaster Square,Callander in the Trossachs.*
*Rob Roy, a former cattle farmer, died in 1734.*
*His grave lies behind Balquhidder church.*

# CHAPTER SEVEN

## *Highland Hunting Lodge*

Everyone was slightly sleepy at breakfast and black coffees were handed around first, followed by a large and welcome meal, to start the day.

The sun had been shining for hours as we left Edinburgh at 9am heading for the Forth Road Bridge.

We had packed overnight cases. An air of excitement rippled through the coach. We were, at last, off to the Highlands and who knows what strange happenings.

John Watson, sitting beside me, was particularly chatty.

'I feel we have all been travelling for weeks, not just days' he confided.

'Yes. We all seem to get along rather well.'

Dolly, two seats ahead, turned and smiled happily.

Exactly across the aisle sat Jill, whom I now felt that I knew especially well. We had had many chats in the evenings at the hotel. And we seemed to click.

Right now she was busy with a map trying to trace the route we would be taking. I decided not to interrupt.

'I wonder how long it will take to get to Braemar?' asked John.

Jill heard. And had the answer all ready. 'About three hours or maybe four if we stop once or twice.'

'Is that where we are spending the night?' she asked John.

'Somewhere not far away from Balmoral Castle, the Queen's Scottish residence. She may be there. This is the time of year when the Royal family take their annual Scottish holiday.'

Dolly turned round instantly. 'Do you mean we may even see the Queen?' She sounded amazed.

'It's possible. We'll buy a Scotsman newspaper or a Times and check out if she has arrived yet.'

Dolly's face was rapt at the thought of being able to return to New York and state that she had actually seen Queen Elizabeth.

I could well imagine it would be enough to keep anyone - let alone a well travelled New Yorker like Dolly - with enough dinner party material to be invited out for at least a year.

I smiled and listened to John who was keen to explain to Dolly a little more about the Royal family's Scottish holiday.

'The grouse shooting season opens on 'the glorious twelfth' August 12, a big event in Scotland. 'The Royals' like to be here hunting and fishing at this time of the year.'

'The Queen still rides and her mother, the Queen Mother, now an amazing centenarian, used to fish for salmon in her long rubber waders, on the River Dee, near Balmoral Castle, until she was in her eighties.'

By now not only Dolly, but everyone was listening. Charles Edward York had paused in the aisle as he went by to speak to Dr Hamish Craig. They talked history a lot. But obviously this present-day history was fascinating too.

John's snippets about our Royal family most foreigners love to hear.

Don and Dorothy Oldenshaw, in the seats just ahead, were listening intently.

John paused.

'Do tell us more' said Dorothy suddenly.

John looked a trifle embarrassed. He had not intended to launch into a Royal family lecture. However he said with a twinkle in his eye 'We'll know if we see them on the moors. They usually have 4 x 4 Land Rovers. Sometimes the Queen pops into the local shops in Ballater, just like the rest of us.'

There was an indrawn gasp from Dolly and an 'oooh' from someone just ahead of her.

Charles Edward smiled and said with a broad wink 'Now it's becoming a Royal tour.'

'Do you know that Charles believes he may be related to Bonnie Prince Charlie, the Young Pretender to the throne of Scotland?' I said to all who were listening.

Dolly, the Oldenshaws and Jill all smiled and nodded They liked the affable, educated young man from

Toronto. He had a certain style about him. They could see that his 'slim chance' of Royal connections through his family name, might well in fact be true.

John said quietly 'If you'd like to know how the Royal family came to have beautiful Balmoral Castle in Deeside, we'll discuss it at dinner tonight.'

'That's a splendid idea' I said. Everyone agreed.

Charles Edward found his seat just behind us and leaned forward with a smile. 'I've researched quite a lot more and Dr Craig has kindly loaned me a history book or two.'

John penned a small note and handed it across to me. 'I'd quite forgotten how much interest our Royal family provokes with tourists.'

I nodded and smiled. We settled back into the momentum of watching the countryside change and I could feel the far hills beginning to beckon. And a sense of mounting excitement.

Suddenly Ted's cheerful voice crackled over the microphone. 'We'll stop for a breather at the next lay-by. You'll feel the air becoming fresher, and cleaner, as we rise into the hills.'

He was practically reading my mind. I had noted that there were far fewer cars on the road as we skirted the stylish 'fair city' of Perth and went onto the A93. It was like stepping back thirty years. No traffic jams! What bliss.

John stopped studying his map. 'We're making very

good time' he said.

The route north to the winter ski slopes of Glenshee and the Cairngorm Mountains I knew well. Its expansive countryside swoops and stretches as far as the eye can see, an indelible reminder of the glaciers that were once here.

But for me on wintry, spring or summer days it is also the meandering, shallow, tinkling rivulets that send tingles of excitement. Crystal clear, whooshing over bright round pebbles, you can count the plump, silvery fish.

I had never seen rivers that run so fast as those in Scotland. Would they still, I wondered? Falling from the stark mountains above.

I was lost in my daydreams as the coach pulled in.

We piled out and gasped the fresh air. It was like intoxicating wine.

'We're heading for a hotel near the Spittal of Glenshee' said Ted, 'Glenmorchie House. It's surrounded by moors and the mountains. The food is excellent and the atmosphere..' he laughed. ' Just wait until you see the place.'

Curiosity buzzed around us. We all had questions to ask but no-one knew how to frame them.

Dolly piped up 'Will we be near Balmoral tonight?'

'Not too close, but tomorrow we shall be. We're at the magnificent hunting     lodge where Charles Edward Stuart, that's Bonnie Prince Charlie..' Ted paused and looked across at Charles Edward to make sure he was listening '..took cover following his flight from Culloden.' He smiled quickly. 'Well, that's as legend has it.'

Charles Edward Lord was standing right behind me. I heard him murmur something agreeable to Dr Craig.

John was listening intently.

'Note the weather, perfect for walking, if you've a mind to' said Ted looking up at a shimmering blue sky.

There was a general sigh of appreciation.

Late August and early September are some of the finest months of the year in the Highlands with the heather still on the hills, transforming them into shades of soft and enticing purple, pink and lilac.

It was a beautiful sight, only rarely captured on photographs. At first glance the haze looks like mist on the moors as the tough Scottish heather gives up its ruggedness, and looks just like a country garden.

Now the sun was high in the sky.

'I could sit and enjoy the scenery and listen to the birds singing all day' said Ted, as he sat down beside me on a grass and rocky ledge that somehow seemed built to sit upon. 'It's a little bit of heaven, that's what I think.'

I grinned. And nodded. 'Is Glenmorchie House like that too?'

He leaned forward, confidingly 'No. It has a terrible history.' His face darkened for a moment.

I had never seen Ted look even remotely grim. But he

did now. I shuddered.

'How?'

'It was owned by a laird of the Campbell clan in the 1600's. And had a dark reputation for plunder and murder. Then it was partly burnt down half a century later. It was re-built for the Stuarts, the Royals in the early 1700's. It's after that, that Bonnie Prince Charlie stayed there, they say. It stood unoccupied for half a century, following Culloden.

'The property was inherited in 1868 and turned into a hunting lodge. That how it stayed until the 1960's when the owner's daughter took over the estate but she didn't want to live there. She re-developed it into a hotel. It's been that ever since, very successfully.'

He leaned closer to my ear. 'They say that the place is the most haunted hunting lodge in Scotland.'

I think I must have shivered because Ted looked sideways at me and half smiled.

'But that's it's big attraction. The ghosts are what tourists like.'

By now I was pulling a face.

'Hope I get an un-haunted room.'

'Don't worry. Most of these things are legends and myths but I'll have a word with Jenny to make sure you don't get Room 301. That's palatial. And for various reasons we try to keep it unoccupied.'

Ted was hardly being helpful.

'Mary, Queen of Scots slept there,' he said suddenly

heaving himself up from the grass. And deciding we must all go.

Suddenly clouds swept across the sky. I looked up and saw a golden eagle whirling far above overhead like an omen. I pointed it out to Jill.

Ten minutes later, having stretched our legs and filled our lungs, we were snuggled back into the coach and moving again.

Ted's voice came over the microphone. 'We'll head on past the Spittal of Glenshee and arrive at Glenmorchie so that we can all have a quick bite to eat and look around while the sun is still shining.'

We all murmured appreciatively.

Jill sat beside me now. She seemed rather excited. 'I wonder that Ted hasn't already told us. You know the pretty film star who lost her jewellery at the hotel, well, part of her film The Vampire of Glas Shiel, was shot at Glenmorchie House, only last year.'

She showed me the reference in a very up-to-the-minute tourist guide.

'Gosh' I said, now just as curious as Jill. 'Does it say anything about Mary, Queen of Scots?'

Jill was busily reading on. And then stopped, startled.

'Yes, it does. It seems she stayed here on her last night in Scotland before, well, before travelling to …'

'…her death?'

'Yes, though it was several months later' said Jill almost re-assuringly. 'The place has quite a bleak

83

history.   From the days of the uprisings and Bonnie Prince Charlie.'

'Wonder why we are staying there?'

'It's a hotel these days.'

'What a history though' I added.  'I think we should tell Charles Edward the involvement the Stuarts had with it.'

Jill was already passing her tourist guide two seats back to the young Canadian.

The coach was heading nearer and nearer to the Highland hotel. Suddenly a sense, not of excitement, but apprehension gripped me for the first time.

Outside the mountains rolled into the far distance, the glen opened wide and free ahead and the rivers danced. Yet my forbodings would not go away.

Could the missing diamonds from our Hollywood starlet be connected in any way to this strange, uncomfortable-sounding hunting lodge with its gloomy past? Could we be heading not for an adventure but for some other excitement: one that we did not really seek? I dare not voice my feelings or thoughts to Jill, just in case by speaking them they somehow became true.

Instead when Charles Edward leaned forward to thank Jill and exclaim that this was an amazing coincidence, I could only smile and wonder if it was.  Or whether fate had dealt us some strange hand.

'Are you OK?' said Jill perceptively.

I brightened up.         'Yes, absolutely fine.  I was just

wondering when we would arrive.'

At that, again almost on cue, Ted said over the microphone. 'Another ten minutes. We turn left and along a very long private drive.' Then he added with a laugh. 'I'll drop the speed so that you don't feel the bumps. The view is worth every second of the way.'

I could already hear cameras being reached for and their snap, snapping as the scenery became wilder and more rugged. Don Oldenshaw was video-filming while his wife did the camera shots.

'It's the most fantastic scenery' I heard Dorothy say. She was obviously enjoying the grandeur of the Cairngorm Mountains.

We negotiated Devil's Elbow, a sharp bend shaped like a bended elbow, that blocks regularly every winter from the swirling snow as it covers the glen and whirls across the fields. As well as rising fast into the mountains this road was quite tricky for a coach.

Ted was being careful not to wander off the main highway for fear of sinking into the peat on either side. I was keeping an eye on it too, remembering that even car drivers did this occasionally. And found they went down into the soft verges with amazing speed.

But Ted knew exactly what he was about.

More slowly now we climbed the gradient towards this sweeping and almost desolate mountain range.

There was an eerie silence as everyone looked and said nothing in their delight and awe. Only the cameras made any sound. And the comforting purr of the coach engine, now dropped into second gear.

Seven minutes later we were off the main A93 and, as Ted indicated, on a slightly bumpier ride.

This was an adventure. We were game for anything.

One mile along the road Glenmorchie House appeared, looking proud and sombre and as though its woodwork held a thousand secrets.

It was both impressive and dramatic with turrets and a small tower at the rear. It looked more like a castle than a hunting lodge.

And it was absolutely huge. I was totally unprepared for its size. Later I was to see that it was a full six stories high and had corridors and rooms that had long since existed to be in everyday use.

Ted pulled the coach right up to the front door. The entrance was under a crenellated large stone storm porch.

If we were stepping back a hundred or five hundred years, there seemed to be little difference. For me, and most others in the coach party, Glenmorchie House seemed very historic; very old. And not a little frightening.

A set of bagpipes rested beside the unopened front door plus boots, gaiters and oiled rainmacs and hoods.

Ted wrestled with the front doors, albeit unsuccessfully, when a man in his seventies came out from a side entrance. He was clad in a kilt, sporran and a tweed jacket. And wore heavy brogues. He carried a key that was at least six inches long. And looked heavy.

Yet he was nimble and quickly opened the front door.

'Miss Jenny is taking a rest. She didna' expect ye until four' he said in a broad Scots accent 'But welcome.. welcome to Glenmorchie.'

Ted nodded and smiled. And thanked the man whom we were later to learn was Jock McAllister, the handyman and gamekeeper on the estate.

He looked tough, rather wizened. And no-one's fool.

Behind the smile there was a wariness, I noted.

Several cars were on the car park. A large new Mercedes and a very stunning sports car, a Porche. Plus two other vehicles and a large long white van that looked almost new.

A small green van with Glenmorchie House on the side, the words in fancy gilt writing, stood some distance away; obviously their own 'fetch and carry' transportation. I imagined that freezers would always need to be filled and essential items collected from the big towns, either from Perth or Aberdeen.

It was with a sense of relief that I realised we were not the only guests.

John was alongside as we stepped inside. He touched my arm. 'What a strange and fascinating place.'

I nodded.

Just then the sound of bagpipes began to waft in from the open air. Through the casement window from the high, vaulted entrance foyer, Jock could be seen playing a Highland tune.

He was obviously welcoming us.

The reception desk was in dark polished mahogany, and suddenly Jenny appeared, smiling and talking quickly.

She was in her fifties, small, round, vivacious, with dark brown curly hair and big laughing dark eyes. I imagined she had been quite 'a bombshell' in her time. Most men would still think of her as comely.

And she was not the least bit Scottish. At least she had no noticeable accent. I couldn't help seeing that she wore the most magnificent diamond and emerald ring on her left hand, plus a wedding band. So she must be married.

At that I became slightly cross with myself. I was not a detective. What on earth was I doing even noticing such things?

Probably Jenny had a perfectly super husband who would emerge later. And even if he didn't show up, it was certainly none of my business.

Nearer the truth is that I had expected her to be dowdy; or at least clad in tartan skirt, cashmere and with a plain hair style. But she was almost glamorous. Somehow it took me by surprise.

She was talking to me. Jill gave me a big nudge and said 'Would you like the turret? I gather it's splendid.'

I half blushed and nodded 'Yes, lovely, thank you.'

Jenny handed me a key. And suggested I sign the hotel

reception book later.

I turned to Jill. 'Where are you?'

'Room 29, literally underneath your room, so you can tap on the floor if you have a message.'

At that we both laughed. And Jenny smiled too.

She was already looking at John and suggesting he should have an adjacent room.

'In the East Wing. It's very comfortable, and close to the magnificent library.'

'That will do me very well. Can I use the library?' said John, seizing the opportunity.

'Yes, of course. It is usually locked but I will arrange for you to have a key.'

Jenny was being charming, efficient and hospitable; a perfect hostess.

John turned to Charles Edward, who was bringing his case in. 'Charles, there's a good library here. Stay in the East Wing if you can. We can do some research.'

Charles Edward looked surprised and delighted. But found that he had been allocated another room.

It was in the North Wing.

'I'm sorry. It's just the way it works' said Jenny.

'Armed with a map, I'll find you John, never fear, he said flippantly, adding quietly 'This is a huge place isn't it?'

It was arranged by Ted that we would all meet in the Long Lounge for a snack. And so that we would converge and get the layout of the house.

Half an hour later Jill and I looked in. The lounge was beautiful, with paintings of Bonnie Prince Charlie on the panelled oak walls and high, high ceilings that went up, it seemed, almost to the sky. We were alone.

Ted appeared, looking worried. 'Do you think everyone else has fallen asleep?' He dashed off to find them.

A side table was prepared for our lunch. We helped ourselves to smoked salmon, tiny brown rolls and a glass of dry white wine. Then followed with cheese from the board and salad. I had a slice of the most gorgeous coffee/chocolate gateau and then a small black coffee.

'Shall we explore outside?' said Jill.

'Yes, of course. But where is everybody?'

I was about say more when something, or rather someone, caught my eye.

It was the young porter who had helped with our cases at The Deerstalker. He was walking past the open door with a colleague and wore a smart dark suit, his fair hair slicked back. But it was his voice that first attracted my attention.

That was it. The voice I had heard at 2am on the night of the jewel robbery in Edinburgh. The voice I had told the police I would 'know anywhere'.

I listened as hard as I could. And then the young men walked in. There was no doubt in my mind this was him. The voice and intonation was exact.

When he saw Jill and I, he looked startled, mumbled

some brief excuse and left very fast.

'What was all that about?' asked Jill. 'Do you know him?'

'Oh dear' I said sitting down suddenly, feeling faint. 'Yes, and no.'

Then I collapsed in a heap.

## CHAPTER EIGHT

### *A Bonnie Prince*

I was in the turret room with its dove blue curtains and soft carpets of royal blue strewn with pink roses when I awoke. It was daylight. A note lay on my bedcover.

> 'We were worried about you. Dr Craig
> said that a rest in your room was the
> best thing. Hope you feel better now.
> Love, Jill'

It all came flooding back to me. I had to see John and tell him, before anyone else.

A large jug of fresh orange juice was on the bedside table. I helped myself. And lay back on the pillows feeling refreshed.

There was a gentle tap, tap on the door and Jill popped her head in followed by Dolly and Dorothy.

'Hi, you're awake. Good' said Jill.

They all quietly came into the large square room with its wall hangings and paintings of Highlanders.

'Yes. And I'm feeling fine. I'm sorry about fainting.'

'You gave us such a shock' said Dorothy, sitting herself on the end of the wide bed with Dolly beside her.

'Ted sends his best wishes and so does Dr Craig. The doctor says he'll have a quick word with you later but he's sure there's nothing for you to worry about.'

I smiled and sipped my drink and thanked them. 'Is John about?'

'Last seen in the library surrounded by a huge pile of books' said Dorothy 'Shall I get him? It's just across the hall.'

'Well, it can wait a few minutes. I want him to know what made me collapse. He might like to investigate.'

They looked curious.

'Yesterday I told the police that I would know the voice I heard at The Deerstalker in the early hours on the night of the jewel robbery.'

They all nodded and listened intently.

'Well, that's what I heard. The same voice' I laughed nervously. 'Then I had to spoil it all by fainting.'

Jill said incredulously. 'You mean it was one of those young men who walked in? I remember what happened'

'Yes. Andy, I think his name is. He worked on our first night at The Deerstalker. He was carrying our cases.'

Jill looked astonished. 'When he saw you he fled!'

I smiled and nodded. I was still feeling a little fragile. 'It was almost as though 'he knew that I knew'. He guessed that I recognised his voice. That was enough.'

'Yes' said Jill to Dolly and Dorothy. 'He simply rushed off when he saw Amy. It was obvious he did not wish to be confronted.'

'I think his mind was reading my mind. Bit like thought transference. He felt guilty. Quite odd really.' I said, adding 'John, as a detective, will know what to do next.'

They all agreed.

'By the way, let's keep this just to ourselves and John. And don't, don't tell Ted, not at this stage anyway. It would be awful to spoil the tour, especially now we are in the Highlands. And anyway my gut feelings may all be quite wrong.'

Jill poured me another orange and helped herself and Dolly to small glasses of the juice. Dorothy rushed off to look for John.

John arrived, carrying a large book. And looking very studious.

'Glad to hear you are feeling better, Amy. 'I believe you have something about the robbery to tell me.'

I explained, keeping it brief.

He nodded and paced the room. 'A voice can be a complete giveaway, almost as distinctive as D.N.A.; people never seem to realise it.'

He was immediately into action mode. And put his big leather bound book to one side. 'Right. I'll try to locate his connection with The Deerstalker. He may wish to keep that secret. If he's involved with the jewellery

robbery, he most certainly will.    If he's innocent,'
John continued 'then he's likely to talk about working
there and we can assume he has nothing to hide.'

'Did you know our robbery was in today's Scotsman?'
said Dolly in her laconic New York drawl. 'The paper
was in the lounge. I was reading it because Ted said
we would know if the Queen was at Balmoral from the
Royal diary they publish daily.'

'What did it say?' we all gasped at once.

'There was something about spreading the police
inquiry to Aberdeen.'

John smiled. 'That's strange. We're not far from
Aberdeen. What else?'

'Sorry. Once I realised they had not caught the thieves I
lost interest.'

'We must get hold of a copy. Also let's make a point of
catching up on the local television news at 6pm.'
Everyone agreed.

'I'll go down now and see what I can find out. It's
already five o'clock' said John. 'This evening looks as
though it could be exciting. See you downstairs.' With
that he was off.

'He's a very eager detective' said Jill.

When we met again it was in the long bar with its
dozens of different whiskies, many bottled by local
distillers. We were invited to visit them all to see the
golden liquid being produced.

John had changed into a dark green velvet smoking

jacket and sported a  Royal Stuart tartan bow tie which he said he had spotted in one of the Borders gift shops, and decided  he rather liked.  He was certainly blossoming.

Ted arrived wearing  tartan, a grouse claw brooch held a plaid firmly over one shoulder.

Several of us were dying to ask him what it meant. But we  decided to wait until everyone had had a drink or two. It was an Anderson plaid, lots of blue with  touches of red.

When I looked  round there was John with a copy of The Scotsman.  He walked over.

'I've had a word with  the youngster.   He says his cousin works at The Deerstalker  and that they are very alike.  Seems lots of people mix them up.'

'That's a very clever cover.'

John smiled. 'Yes. That's exactly what I thought.  You know you're  a good detective.  He's probably  trying to confuse  us to throw us off  the scent.'

'By the way. There's a  massive £150,000 reward for the return of the jewels. It was on  Scottish TV tonight.'

'Wow' I gasped.  'Have you told the others?'

'Not yet. But  I will. It's worth  spending a few hours of our time looking, don't you think?'

'You mean it would pay for another holiday?'

He nodded  and smiled.  'Exactly.'  Then  suddenly John's face changed and his eyes clouded.

'Have you seen Charles?   He said he'd  see me here at

five. He had found this very old volume about the Stuarts in the library and said he wanted to explore the West Wing.' John was looking worried now and glanced at his watch. 'That was hours ago.'

Ted was beside us, listening now, and was immediately 'on the job'

'Let's see if he's in his room for a start' said our coach driver amiably. He dashed off, tartan swishing out behind him.

It was quite a jolly party at the bar by now with other guests joining the group.

We went over to the long windows to sit, and sink into the comfortable brown leather sofas.

Outside cars were coming and going.

Perhaps it would be busy here tonight. Our own party were crowding together.

Dolly, Jill and Dorothy had heard about the £150,000 reward and were keen to spread the news. After all we were there on the night it all happened. We felt we could be as likely as anyone to find the robbers.

Receptionist Jenny, now changed into an elegant royal blue dress with chiffon over panels, was announcing that dinner would be served in the main banqueting hall at eight o'clock.

'She looks stunning' I said to Jill, and could not help notice that she now wore a superb treble row of pearls around her neck with a sapphire jewel at the centre front.

'She's a strange one, here in the Highlands' said Jill.

I nodded.

At that moment Jenny walked towards me, smiling broadly. 'I heard that you were not well this afternoon. I hope you feel lots better now.'

I thanked her for her concern, and for a second felt slightly annoyed with myself, for resorting to 'being catty'. She was probably just as nice as she looked.

It was then that I noticed something strange. On her left hand third finger she now wore a beautiful diamond and a sapphire ring: the emerald and diamond ring had been replaced.

That the missing jewels were diamonds and sapphires clicked in my brain, almost unconsciously.

Could there possibly be a connection?

When Ted returned he walked over to me. Now he was looking perturbed. 'There's no sign of Charles in his room. Do you think he could have gone out for a walk?'

Suddenly John re-appeared with Don Oldenshaw and Dr Craig. But no one had seen Charles, our Bonnie Prince Charlie seemed to have vanished.

'What about outside?' said Don.

'I'll get Jock to scout around in case he's taking a wander on the estate' added Ted.

'Charles is a big, tough guy. I'm sure he can take care of himself' said our Texan rancher. 'But if we're mounting a search party count me in.'

John and Hamish Craig included themselves in this. We had to do something to locate our friend.

Ted murmured and nodded his thanks, adding 'I'll organise a quick search of the house first. It's very easy to get lost in this maze. I've done it myself once or twice.'

~ ~

Charles Edward was in the library standing before a 12ft high oil painting of Bonnie Prince Charlie.

Was this his ancestor ?

Apart from small pictures in tourist guides this was his first real encounter with the style and countenance of the man.

He had spent the afternoon looking through the massive library. And there was much about the original house, the Stuarts and the Prince's eventual downfall at the Battle of Culloden.

The Prince had taken shelter here at Glenmorchie House for several days and nights after escaping from the battlefield with his trusty retainers.

Exhausted, ill, and knowing there was a £30,000 ransom on his head put there by the English King, he had lain low pondering his escape.

Charles clasped the large book to his chest. He started to pace the room, with its parquet floors and long window drapes.     And suddenly he was back there in 1746 re-living Bonnie Prince Charlie's dilemma. It was dynamic. Real history!

The glimpse of light caught his eye beside a heavy woven drape. Wondering if it was a window he leaned forward to look closer. He caught his right foot on the edge of the rug and was flung against the wall, when suddenly the whole room seemed to be moving.

Still clutching, now even more fiercely, the book he was studying, Charles rolled over and over down a stairway.

The steady incline meant there was no way he could stop until he reached the end.

It was pitch black. And where on earth was he?

Amazed and not a little scared, though he would be the last to admit it, Charles grasped a piece of furniture that felt like a wooden chair and pulled himself up off the floor.

His eyes began to get used to the light. The room was like a boudoir. There seemed to be no windows. A small four poster double bed took up most of the space. There was a writing table and chair. It seemed comfortable but not extravagantly furnished.

And a full length painting of an intelligent looking girl of about eighteen, with red hair, dominated one wall.

He wondered. Could it be the young Mary, Queen of Scots and was this her secret room that he had literally stumbled upon? Charles put down the book he was still holding, onto a small table.

It was, he decided, definitely a female's room and quite charming.

He looked around. There were candles and matches. He finally lit a candle and it spluttered to life.

Now, how to get out of the secret room, he wondered. Try as he might he could not see an exit. Or even detect the way he had arrived. Charles pushed and pulled every panel of every wall and nothing moved. He was trapped!

He sat down on a velvet cushioned chair and glanced at his watch.

He had told John he would meet him at 5pm in the lounge. It was now nearly that. John would raise a search party, he was certain. And he settled down to read his book, all about the Stuarts.

It was fascinating. The more he read, the more he felt that they were truly his natural ancestors. Charles was excited by these facts.

He read for one hour, two hours, three hours and finally, exhausted, he fell asleep… and the candle burnt down and went out.

When Charles awoke it was 10.30pm.

Little did he know it then, but around him the whole house was in uproar.

## CHAPTER NINE

*The Vampire of Glas Shiel*

John was near the grand staircase, resplendent with its solid dark oak pillars, like huge square tree trunks, and enormous portraits that seemed larger than life and swept from first floor to the ceiling far above.

He was determined to look inside the large studded door marked in black lettering; PRIVATE. No one else was about. He tried the heavy wrought iron handle. To his surprise it swung open. Quickly he slipped inside.

Dr Craig, Don and Harry Sparrow, and other members of the coach tour had split into two parties; one led by Ted who was touring the stables and farm sheds, the other in the West Wing, where John recalled that Charles had said he might venture.

Darkness had fallen earlier than usual for late August, due to a gathering storm. Outside it was raining. And the winds becoming high.

Everyone was quietly fearful. What if Charles had ventured out into the hills and mountains? But why would he?

Jenny was told that no-one in the coach party would eat

until Charles had been found. She was rather miffed at this but then tried to put on a show of understanding.

'I really do wonder about her after that 'outburst' said Jill.

I too was watching her with much interest.

Jenny had said that there was no chance of serving 'the banquet', as she referred to our evening meal, later than planned, as the staff had to go home at 11pm. And were not likely to be able to stay late.

I had raised my eyebrows adding 'Then we'll serve ourselves. And wash up afterwards.'

At this, obviously not knowing what to say, she turned and excused herself.

'Well, that's settled then' said Jill with a big grin. 'They can hand the meal over to us.'

I nodded. 'Yes. Why ever not. We can do that easily' Then my thoughts darkened again. 'But we do need to find Charles first.'

It brought us both back to earth with a resounding bump.

'I do hope he's OK. There's not an ounce of harm in that young man.'

Jill nodded.

'John has put out a call to get his mobile phone number from Toronto. He may have his phone with him and be unable to ring out.'

'Gosh. Where is John?'

'Well, he said he was vanishing for a few minutes.

103

'There's something he wants to check out on the first floor, a room I believe.'

I looked at Jill with what must have appeared to be alarm. Not another of our bunch about to disappear.

Jill laughed. 'Don't worry. He is, after all, a detective.'

'A very real Sherlock Holmes' I said with an element of truth.

'Yes, of course. I'd quite forgotten that. Well we can certainly do with his help the way things are turning out on this adventure.'

We picked up a copy of The Scotsman and there was more about the missing jewels, on the front page.


'POLICE HUNT SWITCHES TO BRAEMAR' was the headline. And Jill started to read aloud 'The missing Dechter diamonds, part of a valuable family heirloom belonging to Swiss aristocrats, on loan to US film company, Executive Cine, and worn by the star Gloria Franklin, at the Scottish film premiere of The Vampire of Glas Shiel, shown at The Edinburgh Festival this week, are being sought in the Braemar area. The jewels were snatched from an Edinburgh hotel.

'Police have set up road patrols. Aberdeen's Dyce airport has brought in plain clothes police and extra customs officers.

'The search is made more difficult due to the volume

of visitors expected in the area when the Royal Family arrives for its annual Scottish holiday, later today. The reward offered by Executive Cine has been increased to £200,000'

'Oh, I must tell Dolly - they're arriving!' said Jill excitedly, referring to the Royals.

She handed me the paper. And dashed off to find our New York friend, Dolly, who was getting her coat, rainhat and some stout shoes before joining the outdoor hunt for Charles.

I tucked the paper under my arm knowing that I must find John to tell him the latest news.

Either we were at the very heart of the robbery, here at Glenmorchie House. Or we were not very far away.

After all The Vampire of Glas Shiel had been filmed here. What better place to 'hide up' with the missing jewels.

Maybe Charles had unwittingly stumbled across something when he was in the library; something that meant he had to be kept 'out of the way' until the jewel thieves were safely out of the country with their haul.

My mind was rushing, leaping ahead. And shouldn't we be informing the police that Charles was missing. That thought had occurred to me earlier. But now, in the light of the newspaper story, maybe we should. Perhaps he was in real danger. We could not leave it a moment longer.   Supposing he was still missing by tomorrow.!

John appeared five minutes later. He looked   weary, I thought.

I showed him The Scotsman. 'I think  something strange is going on here, don't you?'

'Yes. I do.   I've been inside a room that is full of recent documentation about the film.     And   I have some names and addresses that may be useful to the  police.'

'Shall we ring them?'

'I've already  done  so.     Chief  Inspector   Alastair McIntyre of the CID is due here  in about twenty five minutes.'

'Have you told him about Charles?'

He nodded. 'I felt  I should.  We can't let  him down.'

'The  Inspector  was  quite  interesting.     He  said that Glenmorchie  had a very  strange reputation.'

'In what way?'

John   leaned towards me.  'He said two  years ago a gang of thieves holed out here all winter.  There were grave suspicions of money laundering  and much more. When the police swooped they had  upped and gone just hours before.'

My eyes opened wide. I went on listening.

'It was after the house 'hit the headlines' so to speak that the film makers 'discovered' this place. And then decided to use it to make their film, Vampire of  Glas Shiel.'

It was all a surprise.

'The Inspector is bringing with him a copy of the film. And intends to show it tonight. He says it will show the layout of the house and could help us find Charles.'

None of this was making sense. I must have looked totally perplexed.

John continued. 'There are all sorts of lower tunnels and hideaways and maybe even areas that cannot be reached except through secret doors, including Royal apartments. Anyway this was explored in the film, by...'

.. the vampire?' I said suddenly, quite horrified.

'Yes. But how did you know?' John was almost hopping with excitement. "You link things up - automatically. The instinctive mind...'

'Well, thank you. There's something I want to mention about Jenny and her jewels before your friend the Inspector arrives, in case I forget later. She's wearing sapphires and diamonds tonight.'

He looked very surprised. 'I'll order us a pot of tea and you can tell me while we wait to meet the police' With that John dashed off to ring a bell for service.

Half an hour later the two search parties returned bedraggled and wet; they had nothing new to report. Except that Ted said, with an air of gloom, that the coach had 'a flat' on the front driver's side. It would have to be repaired.

But luckily he had his spare tyre and had checked: it

was perfect. Harry Sparrow, a mechanic as it turns out, said he would be delighted to assist, as did John, Don and even Dr Craig.

'We're covered by the A.A. I'll ring them first.' said Ted.

But everyone said if he had the wheel changing gear surely it was not so different from a car.

'A little heavier' quipped Ted, brightening up and adding his thanks. 'We'll look at it in daylight and decide. I've never had a complete flat tyre before. It's a bit strange.'

We nodded in unison.

'The place seems spooked' said Dolly who had now appeared, having taken off her wet outer clothes and left them in the storm porch.

'Maybe that's why they made 'the Vampire' film here' I said. Obviously the thought of seeing it was uppermost on my mind.

It was not the right thing to say. I realised it the moment it had slipped out. We had not yet slept here and while none of us were easily scared, that did not mean we felt quite at ease either. Charles had effectively disappeared. Now the coach was immobilised.

After removing their dripping wet macs and boots everyone decided a whisky, preferably with Crabbie's ginger wine added - to give it extra heat - was a very good idea.

'We'll do this 'on the company' said Ted. And went

towards the bar to start ordering.'

Everyone found a space and sat down wherever they could, on chairs, bar stools and some on the carpet, to decide what we would do next. It was like a war council.

Charles, our likeable young 'Bonnie Prince Charlie' was, after all, still missing. No one felt the least bit hungry. But we were alarmed.

I was already wondering when the Inspector would arrive. It was at least forty minutes since John had mentioned it.

At that moment there was a call into the hotel for John.

We sipped our drinks. The combination of Highland malt whisky and Crabbie's Scots ginger was certainly like fire in our tummies. And would also help to settle our nerves.

'Not good news' said John when he returned. 'The Inspector can't come. He won't see us now until the morning.'

'And Charles?' I blurted out.

'He is biking the film out to us and suggests we watch it tonight. And that I ask him questions tomorrow. I now have Charles' mobile phone number to try, from the Toronto exchange.'

John took out his own mobile phone and was already tapping the number in.

We all waited in trepidation.

'It's ringing' said John quietly.

Everyone held their breath, listening.

His face fell suddenly. 'It's coming up with an answerphone .' He clicked it off.

'Leave a message' squeaked Jill, who was sitting beside me.

'OK. What shall I say?'

'Just ask him where he is and to call back. Give him your mobile number '

There was a general murmur of agreement.

John tapped the numerals in and waited for the message to repeat. Suddenly his faced changed into astonishment. He heard Charles.

'Charles, it's John here; John Watson. Where are you? We're looking for you. Can you call us on 03176 392180?'

He listened quietly, then said 'I heard his voice. He's in the house somewhere.'

'Try again' said Don. 'Did he sound OK?'

John was already tap-tapping the numbers in again. 'Well. It was definitely him but it was very feint. He must be exhausted.'

Now everyone was quietly murmuring to each other. John listened as the telephone rang. It switched into answerphone. 'If you hear this Charles, it's John on 03176 392180. Call me, and don't worry.. we'll be with you asap.' He put the phone down on the small table and paced up and down.

Then he started to explain about the film made at the

hotel.   And  the reason why  we would be watching it.
Outside there was the  roar  of the  motor bike arriving.
A  police  rider  in  helmet,  black  leathers  and  gaiters
walked into the foyer carrying a  small parcel.
'Mr Watson?'  His voice had a strong Scottish burr.
John  moved  swiftly  forward  taking  the  parcel  and
signing  for  it.  'Thankyou.  Will  you be seeing  the
Inspector later?'
The  young man    hesitated.   He walked carrying his
large black helmet in one hand. 'Probably not, sir.'
'Well, if you do, thank him for  his speed.'
'Aye  sir.  It's all in there, with instructions.'
'We have the film of The Vampire of  Glas Shiel' said
John holding the package aloft, as the  young biker  left
the room.
'Now  we  need  to  get  Jenny  to  let  us   see  it  in  the
conference room. Maybe we  make some sense of this
large house with its secret passages and find Charles.'
'Shall I  ask  her?' I said jumping up.
John nodded. 'Don't for goodness sake  say which film
we are watching.    Just ask if we can run 'a film'.  He
smiled.
Which meant he certainly didn't trust Jenny. Any more
than I did.
Twenty minutes later we were all waiting for the  film
to start. The large room, with all  cinema facilities, had
been used by the  American company for editing and
cutting  during the  making of 'Vampire of Glas Shiel'.

111

A short cover story board accompanied the film. John read it aloud to us in the semi-darkened room.

'The film is    part fantasy. A young American guy in his twenties, arrives in the Scottish Highlands, hoping to trace his ancestors, but finds himself    acting strangely.    He    begins    to feel he has supernatural powers.

'On the night of the full moon, he turns into a vampire, complete with a ferocious mouth and red staring eyes. A likeable easy going youngster, he is unaware of what is happening.

'Then he reads of the ancient curse of Glas Shiel ..'

John's voice began to falter. He stopped reading and paused to look across the room.

No one said a word, though we all felt deeply worried, uncomfortable.

The film was now rolling, starting with the credits. Everyone watched in total silence. First the outdoor shots of the Grampians and Glenshee, then straight to the hall of Glenmorchie House, the foyer and the young screen hero; American Brad Walker.

There was a gasp from John as he recognised the magnificent library and saw Brad open a book to research his family history.

Suddenly the young man is whirling about. He slides and falls, and falls - and lands in another totally historic apartment.

But what has happened?

John jumped up and switched on the lights. 'That's it. Where I left Charles earlier today in that very room - the library, researching his ancestors!'

Everyone looked stunned. The film had only been running for five minutes.

'I believe he has fallen into the sealed room - the Royal apartments. If we pause the film we can look in the library now.'

As one, everyone jumped up and followed him out of the room, up the grand staircase to the library.

'Could it be Room 301?' I whispered to Ted as he passed me, remembering his earlier warning about it.

He stopped for a moment. 'That was a more recent happening - but I'll check it out.'

John opened the door and hinges creaked eerily. Inside pitch black, he searched for a switch but could find none. Through the wide and high windows the moon was shining.

As ever, practical Jill found light switches at waist level and switched them on one by one. Chandeliers began to light up the stunning, old, faded, still grandoise room, with its shelves ceiling high, lined with hundreds of books.

No one else apart from John and Charles, had set foot in the room until now.

'We were right here.' said John. 'I was looking at a Conan Doyle book and Charles, let's see, he was over there and said he had something really amazing; it was all about the Stuarts and Bonnie Prince Charlie.' He walked over to the spot. 'This is exactly where I left him - at about 3 o'clock this afternoon.'

'Shall we try to re-create it?' suggested Ted.

'Reconstruct the crime?'

'Yes, why not?' drawled Don.

'OK. He was standing here reading' John walked about a bit, but nothing happened.

'What we don't know is what made him slip' I said, then noticed the rug was still curled into a dangerous roll on its corner. 'Look. This could be it.'

I paused, with Jill, Dolly and Dorothy beside me. We tried feeling for trap doors, or anything different, with our fingers.

'Do be careful' said Dorothy

'There must be something' suggested Dolly. 'In the film he seemed to fall from about here.'

But there was nothing to be seen or felt except the curled up corner of the slightly threadbare rug.

Little did I know it but I was a fraction away from touching the wall behind the drapes that would send any one of us spinning and whirling to join Charles in his secret hideaway.

'Let's go downstairs and play back that bit of the film again' said John suddenly.

As one, we all trooped down the main staircase. John's phone was ringing. He picked it up quickly and listened. Then his face broke into a broad smile. 'It's

Charles. Are you OK? We think we know where you are.' He was straining to hear. 'Yeah, fine' Then John nodded and closed the phone down.

'The signal was weak but he's all right. Charles says he fell from the library but he doesn't know how. It all happened so fast'.

'I think we've nearly cracked it. Let's just watch the film again from where the American is in the library.'

Someone switched the lights down and the film began to whirr.

At my side Jill said suddenly. 'Do you believe in vampires?'

'No of course not!'

'I've just checked with the paper. It's a full moon tomorrow night.'

'It's just a film' I said. 'A horror movie, it's not true.' I shivered nevertheless.

We were watching the film intently and carefully now. John helped by Dr Craig, turned it back to re-play, at least five times.

The American had simply tripped. Then we noted. He had touched the wall. Maybe that was the clue!

'Shall I go and try it?' volunteered Harry Sparrow, who was emerging as a lively member of the party these days.

'We'll all go' said Dr Craig. Everyone agreed and we rushed back up the staircase.

John paused for a second in the hall. And was using his

mobile.   'I'll ring the Inspector and  see if he can help.'
'Chief Inspector McIntyre  please.'

He waited, listening.

'No-one by that name.  I am through to Aberdeen police
H.Q?'  Now John was  agitated.

Jill, Dolly, Dorothy, Ted and myself - everyone  within
earshot - turned.

'Yes, of course. Sorry to trouble you.'  He clicked off
his phone. A  look of surprise crossing  his face  he
turned to us.   'As you've guessed our  Chief Inspector
was a fake. I wonder why?'

So  who was he? And why did he send us the film?

# CHAPTER TEN

*Who or Why ?*

Walking back up the grand staircase to the library I caught sight of the moon shining brightly through the ornate leaded windows and a shudder ran through me.

The night looked fresh and starry: the high wind had swept away every vestige of the rain and the clouds.

The view from Glenmorchie House was all of mountains and glens lit by the moon.

If not exactly inviting at this time of night, it certainly seemed quite beautiful.

I checked my watch. It was almost 11 o'clock.

Once in the library we tried to action replay Charles' departure but nothing amazing happened.

John called Charles. And was talking quietly.

Then he put the phone down and turned to us. 'Charles says: Thanks for the food.'

'What food?' said Jill.

'Well, it seems a hamper with everything, including drinks, arrived on his floor just ten minutes ago. He didn't even see it arrive. But he's famished, so he's tucking in.'

We all looked at each other, for once lost for words.

'Well, Charles knows we can't get to him yet. But he's OK. I suggest we raid the larder ourselves and then get an hour or two's rest' said John, who now seemed fully in command of the situation.

It seemed a good idea. Though, we knew, it was no solution but we were totally exhausted.

One by one we walked back down the staircase each lost in our own thoughts. At least someone was looking after Charles.

How strange it all was.

I decided to have a further chat with John while we ate, to see if he had brought his 'Holmes-ian' powers of deduction to bear on this latest turn of events.

When we went into the banqueting hall, there, before us, was a thirty foot long table spread with a delectable feast of food. It was a splendid buffet with a handwritten note propped up at the front.

'For the coach party - please help yourselves and enjoy the food and drink.'

'Well' said Dolly beside me. 'Thank goodness. I was beginning to wonder if we were welcome.'

I nodded with a smile.

We moved towards the whole fresh salmon, arranged on a long silver salver, the hams and hot venison, cheeses and freshly tossed salads of every variety. At the far end of the table were raspberry gateaux, fresh cream, fruit salad and chocolate confections. Drinks were on a side table. Plus the coffee was perking and the tea just waiting to be made. Nothing had been forgotten.

Yet there was no sign of anyone, not even Jenny. Maybe, as she said, they had all gone home.

Ted looked both relieved and pleased. At that moment Jock the old Scotsman, walked in, leaning heavily on his stick.

He had a grin that was more like a grimace on his weathered face. He laid his stick to one side, picked up his bagpipes and started to play a Highland reel and his face changed to smiling pleasure.

With wine, whisky and good food before us, we set to, ravenously. We were starving.

What a long, hard and strange day it had been. Though Charles was not with us, at least he had food. And we would get to him in the morning.

'I wonder what on earth is going on here' I said to John between morsels of delicious smoked salmon.

He was eating roast venison with all its trimmings and sipping a glass of red wine.

'I know what you mean. I feel we are being used as pawns in some way.'

'But why?'

'I don't know. Something strange is happening. And our coach party has been chosen to get involved.'

'And why Charles?'

'Good question. Charles is obviously seen as being

119

Bonnie Prince Charlie, the Young Pretender.'

Jill on John's left, was enjoying salad with cold Aberdeen Angus beef. She was listening intently and joined in.

'You know the press are onto to it all. A reporter from the Daily Record in Glasgow rang tonight just before the film started. The police have issued a missing person statement.'

'If one paper has it, they all have' said John with a groan. Then he suddenly brightened up 'Still, maybe that's good. If we can't rescue Charles we'll need their help.'

Harry Sparrow, Dr Craig and Don and Dorothy Oldenshaw walked into the room.

'We've been watching the rest of the film. It's not all horror. It has a happy ending' said Dorothy, finding herself a plate.

'And Gloria, the girl we saw at the hotel, is very charming and a superb actress' added the doctor.

Dorothy continued 'The young American who comes to Scotland to find his ancestors .. and gets into big trouble and has to be rescued. He's just like Charles.'

You could hear a pin drop, it was suddenly so quiet. No-one said a word. Now we were all listening and looking; our senses captured as one.

'We're playing out the film…that's it' said John, sounding alarmed.

'Come and see. It's er, imaginative' said Dr Craig

searching for the right word but not wanting to scare any of us. Everyone left their food and drink.

The sudden blast of bagpipes from Jock, now firmly seated in the corner of the room and determined to stay all night if need be, sounded shrilly through the intrigue.

'Drat those bagpipes' said Dorothy with her Texan drawl. 'I'm not so sure that I like them this much.'

It was a lament. And Jock seemed to be just getting into his stride. The huge house suddenly felt eerie. Outside I noticed that though the moon had moved across the sky, it was still large and seemed to be getting larger.

'Are you coming to watch the rest of the film?' I asked Jill.

'Well, I'm far too petrified to go to my room' she said with a distinct shiver.

'We're exhausted and scared' I said, following everyone else.

There was a resounding knock on the huge outer door. We all jumped, our nerves is disarray, then looked at each other.

Ted strode towards the entrance aggressive and strong, hoping to make us feel better. Did Highland hotels often have visitors in the middle of the night?

It was, predictably, the press, the Daily Express. They were on a hunt for Charles and a story.

Ted let them in; reporter Jack Duncan and

photographer, George   McKay, who had driven up from Edinburgh.    They too looked exhausted. 'Come   in and have a bite to eat  and  a drink' said Ted.

He was going to  tell them the whole thing and hope media coverage would help  us. One thing was certain it couldn't do any harm.

From outside a sudden   sweep of headlights caught in the reflection of  the foyer mirrors.  At least  three cars and  the large white  van that I had seen earlier, were coming onto  the car park.

Other guests, presumably  returning.

Within  seconds the  outside activity had   quietened down. No-one came in through the large front doors of Glenmorchie House.  A few voices  could be heard; a side door slammed. And that was it.

'I did see someone that we  know' said Jill, whispering in my left ear.  'Young Andy from  The Deerstalker, the one who avoided you earlier when you fainted.' And recalling the  incident she added.   'Are you  allright now?'

I nodded and   whispered   back   'Are we actually on holiday? It feels more like being in the middle of a nightmare drama.'

She smiled in agreement. 'Dolly would like very much to go to Braemar and Balmoral, to get a few pictures of the Queen or the  Royal castle.'

When I looked up  at the huge, dominating  16ft portrait of Bonnie Prince Charlie above me,  I was certain that I saw a movement.    I was staring at the man's face, trying to assess if there was any resemblance to Charles, when it happened again.  He winked !

I nearly fell, but hung on tightly to the tall wooden stairpost.

'Gosh, you're not 'going again'? said Jill, seeing my ashen face and reaching to help me.

I collapsed  into an ornate oak  high backed chair and collected myself.  Was I mad? Hallucinating? Or what. Should I tell Jill?

'The man in the portrait  moved' I said, almost lamely. 'He winked.'

Jill looked up. Then back at me.  'If I didn't know you better, Amy, I'd think you'd had one  Drambuie too many.   It's just an oil painting.  How can it move?'

At  that moment all the lights went out!       We were in total blackness, apart from the moon shining in.

Above some  squeals  I heard Ted's re-assuring voice. 'Don't worry. There's a supply of candles here.   I'll light up a few and hand them round. It'll be back on again in a few minutes. They have a reserve generator for emergencies like this.'

But the lights did not go back on. Finally we decided, albeit unwillingly, that it was time for bed. Even the film  could not be finished.  It would have to wait 'til morning.

Ted sorted out rooms for  our new guests, the reporters, and handed them a large, long white candle each.

'Will you sleep?' said Jill to me as we both nervously climbed the staircase, along with everyone else.

Probably; total exhaustion' I said. 'All we need now is ghosts.'

'Shush' she giggled, then murmured 'Sorry, I always seem to giggle when I'm tired and nervous. I'm on the floor below you, and John is just across the main hall.'

'Contingency plans?' I murmured.

Ted was suddenly beside us asking if we would like to be escorted to our rooms. We readily said 'Yes'.

But John was no-where to be seen. I saw a tall lighted candle disappearing into the library along the black corridor. And decided that it was probably John, off on a 'Holmes' trail. He told me earlier that he had found the most amazing information about The Case of the Mysterious Monster by Conan Doyle: he wanted to get back to the library to spend a few more hours researching it before we set off for Loch Ness.

'If we set off' I had said with a half smile.

'Well, yes. But once Charles is recovered we shall.' It was pleasant to hear such firm re-assurance.

John had the shrewd powers and tenacity of a former Met police inspector. He didn't give up. Once on the trail nothing would stop him. I trusted his judgement. What's more I believed he was right in his positive way of thinking and acting.

It was with a lighter heart that I finally tap-tapped a double beat with my shoe, on the floor - for Jill in her room below - to let her know that all was fine at my end. She responded  by  using a long curtain drape rod to tap-tap in reply on her ceiling.

That was our 'all's well' sound.    It suddenly occurred to me that  we had not devised a 'help' signal.

I sank into bed, pulled the soft featherdown  quilt up and over my nose  and I took one more quick look at the moon.    The wide expanse of the windows showed rolling clouds. A swift wind swirled them about and the mountains stayed  sedate,  glorious and cool.    As for the moon:  it  seemed to be smiling.

That night I slept like a log, never dreaming or tossing and turning.  I  awakened to a bright day of sunshine. My alarm clock was shrilly ring-ringing, an imperative summons to the day.

I could already hear  Jock with his bagpipes, outside blaw-blawing, reminding me  that this  was  Scotland.

# CHAPTER ELEVEN

## *The Dechter diamonds*

The morning papers were full of the Charles story.
BONNIE PRINCE CHARLIE GOES MISSING said the normally restrained Scotsman for its second lead front page story. There was a large, and rather handsome, picture of Charles with the words 'Canadian Charles Edward Lord, thought to be a direct descendant of Charles Edward Stuart; Bonnie Prince Charlie. While here investigating his claim to the Scots Stuart lineage he is believed to be held prisoner at Glenmorchie House, Glenshee in the Cairngorms'

The bright and breezy Daily Record announced CAPTIVE BONNIE PRINCE .
It had a sporty rugby playing picture of Charles on their front page and the story outlined the fact that Toronto-born Charles Edward was on a coach trip from England when the Canadian visitor and the whole coach party are believed to have found themselves at the centre of a gang of crooks, trying to steal the Swiss Dechter diamonds and other valuables.

It added 'The Young Pretender' is now lying locked in a secret dungeon being sought by the police while his coaching colleagues try vainly to get to him. He is at Glenmorchie House, the former Stuart Royal hunting lodge, burned down in the 1600's, rebuilt and now a top tourist hotel. Americans and Canadians seriously researching their ancestors, many of whom fled from Scotland following the failed Jacobite Rebellion of 1746, like to stay at Glenmorchie.'

From reading all the news I looked up. Jill was approaching. She was wearing a lovely pastel green cashmere jersey and slim fitting matching trousers.

'You look terrific this morning' I said.

'Well, thank you. I bought these just two days ago, remember? I thought I'd wear them while I'm here.' Then suddenly her mood changed. 'You've seen the papers.'

'Yes, I was just reading them. They've got it all - in one.'

'Absolutely. Let's go through to have breakfast and I'll tell you what's really new.'

We found a small square table which was carefully and prettily set for breakfast with pale blue napkins, shining glasses and chunky beige pottery style china. On the side I noticed the large jugs of fruit juice, plus muesli, cream and milk and a selection of corn flakes, rolls, butter and marmalade all waiting for us to help ourselves.

We seemed to be alone in this large morning room.

'Are we the only one's having breakfast?'

Jill found a seat and helped herself to a hot steaming coffee from the pot that was perking merrily at one end of the side cabinet.

She looked around. 'We seem to be, don't we. I expect the others will be here soon.'

Almost without stopping for breath she added. 'I think they are all in with the police, in the dining room.' She handed me a coffee as I sat awaiting more. 'It seems the police have been watching this place for months. They swooped in the early hours this morning and guess what they found ?'

My mind was still only half awake. I said nothing. It was still only 8.30am; far too early for me to get my mind, or at least the most active part of it, into top gear. I decided to let Jill tell me.

'Charles.. I hope.'

She look thrown by this. And said quickly. 'No, I'm afraid he is still captive but he's been talking to John this morning.' She paused and then continued.

'The police have picked up over £2 million pounds in laundered money here at Glenmorchie. It was hidden in the library.'

'Wow, but who?'

'Well, I gather there was this big money-laundering operation going on all last summer and the Aberdeenshire police just could not get evidence.'

'With the chance to come looking for Charles they issued search warrants and pounced  in the early hours today.'

My mind was now springing into action.  The strong coffee was working wonders.

'And Andy.  Is he involved?'

'He's been taken in for questioning.'  She rushed on, glad of the chance to tell me about it all.  'It seems he is saying he knows nothing.  He didn't even work for the company last summer' she smiled.  'However the police are not so sure.'

'And  Jenny and  the diamonds and sapphires?'

'No news yet.   The real diamonds and sapphires worn in the film by Gloria Franklin  are still missing.'  She leaned forward.  'But it seems there are two fake sets that were made   when the film was first being mooted.  These are  'in circulation' too and  look exceptionally 'real'.

I laughed and put my hand to my mouth.  'How absolutely confusing.'

'Yes.'

Jill added with a smile.  'And before you ask me,  no-one has seen Jenny this morning.    And she is always on duty by  this time.'  She raised  both eyebrows.

'I slept very well last night, unbelievably well' I added, deciding to help myself to some muesli and cream.

'All the kitchen staff are being interviewed.  So no bacon and eggs, I'm afraid.'

I nodded. 'After last night's lovely food I don't think anyone can be hungry.'

Jill agreed. And was soon helping herself to a Continental-style breakfast.

We sat eating quietly, letting the news sink in.

'Have you seen John this morning?'

I had to think our 'Holmes' must be in his element; he was at the heart of such a bizarre and amazing mystery. Now his ex-colleagues, the police were here, too. He would be enjoying every second.

Jill laughed. 'Yes, I ran into him quite by chance in the hall as I came down. He looked totally exhausted. He spent half the night in the library, that is until his candle eventually gutted out. He said he had 'the answer' to his Conan Doyle monster.' She laughed. 'I expect that makes more sense to you than it does to me. Sorry, he asked me to be sure to tell you that. With all that's been going on down here, I quite forgot.'

'What about the newspapers?' I said, picking up The Scotsman again.

'Well, for once they are getting it right. Charles has become an overnight celebrity though I'm not sure he will really enjoy that.'

'It might make it easier for him to trace his lineage.'

She laughed 'That's true.'

'I heard his father is planning to fly into Prestwick today. And will arrive late tonight. He's worried about his son. It's International news, now. I suppose you could call it 'romantic'.

'But no fun for Charles' I said, still worried about the young man we all liked so much. 'I must find out what exactly the police are doing to get him out.'

We heard a noise behind us and an agitated looking Dolly was arriving. She wore a cream beige cardigan, with short sleeves and mid blue coloured trousers and a blouse of soft pink. She looked worried. And carried as well as her handbag, a small parcel; it looked more like a large and rather sturdy envelope.

It was not at all like Dolly to have a frown on her face. Before we could say anything, she said 'Can I pull up a chair?'

'Yes, of course' we both said in unison, reaching for one for her.

She looked shaken, as though she needed a coffee. I went to get one. 'Black or white?'

'Oh thank you, black please' Dolly almost gasped. 'Look what I have here.' She spilled the sparkling contents of the envelope onto the table, between plates and cups and saucers.

'The Dechter diamonds' we gasped.

I put the coffee down on the table.

'I found them in my suitcase, just like this, in this envelope, when I was looking for fresh clothes.'

Dolly's face was ashen. She was scared. 'I didn't put them there' she said, almost like a small child. 'What are they doing in my case, in my bedroom?'

131

'Look, don't worry' I said suddenly. 'They must have been planted on you. Someone has wanted you to bring them here to Glenmorchie. They were probably put into your case at The Deerstalker.'

'Or they could be the fake diamonds. We're told there are some fakes about.' said Jill, thoughtfully. She reached out to touch them, then suddenly pulled back. 'Better not. Fingerprints.'

We nodded.

'When did you last go through your suitcase, Dolly?' I said, adding with a smile. 'Come on. Everyone knows it's not you. Now relax and enjoy your coffee.'

She looked better already. And smiled and began to simmer down. 'Thankyou. It's a good thing you are here or I would not have known what to do.'

She sipped her drink.

'I haven't unpacked my case for a day or so, I guess. You know what it's like..' She was thinking hard. 'We were at The Deerstalker, then Ted said 'pack for two nights away'. She laughed suddenly. 'I just made sure I had undies and a couple of fresh tops and my toilet things and closed the case up again. I never really looked.'

We understood and for a moment wondered, in horror, what we might find when we searched our own suitcases.

'The thing is 'Are they the genuine Dechter diamonds or the fakes?' said Jill.

132

We all looked at the glittering stones lying on the table. None of us were expert enough to know. The gold clasps and the setting of the jewels looked of the highest quality to me. Secretly I thought, these could be the real diamonds and sapphires. I decided not to say so.

'We must find John' I said without another thought.

There seemed to be noises coming from beyond the doors.

'Let's put them back in the envelope.' said Jill, wisely.

Carefully, using a knife, rather than our fingers, we shuffled them into the large padded envelope.

'There. You'd better hang onto them. Tuck them into your bag' I said, just before the door opened and a crowd of people, including the Daily Express men, came in.

They looked across smiling and raised their hands in a wave.

'What shall we do with them?' asked Dolly ruefully.

'Either John or the police will know' said Jill.

'Now, breakfast, Dolly. Muesli with cream; fresh fruit or fruit juice. It's all cold this morning, I'm afraid, due to the general furore.'

Dolly settled for grapefruit first followed by muesli, with fresh cream.

'What about those pictures of the Queen that you need?' I said brightly, hoping to take Dolly's mind off recent events.

'I was on the phone to Madge in New York this morning. I told her I hoped to get some. Do you think we still can?'

'Can't think why ever not.' I said with a smile. 'We all want to go up to Braemar today if we can. Let's find Ted and ask him.'

John appeared and almost on cue Ted followed. You could see that John had been up for most of the night. He looked positively worn out. But was smiling brightly. They came over.

'Good morning, ladies. Hope you slept well.' Ted seemed in great form. 'The good news is that the coach tyre has been replaced, by the A.A. early today. And we are ready to roll, if anyone feels like taking a look at Balmoral and Braemar.'

'Yes, please' we all said with gusto!

'Good' said Ted, delighted. 'We'll leave at ten. Is that OK? Meet you at the front door. Now I've a few things to do first.' He grinned and was off.

John grabbed a nearby chair and after a word with the two newsmen, now enjoying their breakfast, he came over and sat down.

'I'm worried about Charles' I started

He smiled and stopped me while he prepared himself coffee. 'Don't be. He's fine. The police want us to get away from Glenmorchie all day. It's in fact important to see who they can capture and for them to get to Charles if they can.'

'You mean we're in the way.' I half laughed.

'Well, you could put it that way.' He sipped his coffee. 'One of the detectives has just told me that they cannot work out who is lying and who is telling the truth. They need to set up a few traps - and see who takes the bait. Let's say it will be easier with fewer people about.'

'Good' said Jill. 'We can return to being 'on holiday'.

John grinned. 'Yes, as you say. We did have other plans.'

'Are you staying, or coming to Balmoral with us?' I asked.

'I'm coming along too.'

Dolly produced the envelope with the jewels. 'You'd better have these first.'

'Dolly found them in her case, this morning' said Jill.

John took the envelope, carefully peeped inside and his face changed, amazed. 'Well. What can I say. A cool £250,000 there. The police will be delighted.'

'They're real?' we all said as one.

John nodded, pursing his lips thoughtfully.

'I would say so. I've seen quite a few diamonds in my time at the Met. These look genuine. The Dechter diamonds.' He jumped up suddenly. 'I'll hand them to the police now. I'll be right back.'

He left his coffee half finished. And almost ran.

We sat saying nothing.

When John returned he sat down and said. 'Inspector Jackson - the man in charge of this - says he thinks they are real.  He'll need a statement before we set off this morning Dolly, just a brief one about how you found them. Nothing to worry about. You know there's a reward, if they are.'

Over on the far side the reporters were showing interest.

'Don't say anything yet' added John. 'There's a police statement at 11am. They will be told then.'

Two minutes later Dolly was explaining to the police inspector.

At ten o'clock, sharp, we were away, coats and macs in our hands because it looked like rain.  The clouds were swinging across the wide, wide Highland sky and the air was fresh and plentiful.

'Do you know I'm glad to be away from  that place' I said with a shudder.

Glenmorchie?' queried  John who was sitting across the aisle.

I nodded.  'What with its strange name  and  Jock playing his  bagpipes all the time  and that Jenny, it's not my idea of a holiday hotel.'

'Oh, I don't know' said John. 'I've masses of information about  The Case of the Mysterious Monster. It's an amazing  house.'

The coach swung off the  private road and back onto the A93; the almost familiar sweep of mountains and glens stretched around us. Ted switched on the  radio to a lively pop music programme.

John  leaned towards me and whispered. 'I know where

the missing manuscript is.'

I thought that nothing else could surprise me. But I was wrong. This did. It was, I knew, worth more to Sherlock Holmes fans, than the Dechter diamonds, good as their recovery must be. It was a scoop of major importance. And for John his real reason for being on the coach trip.

'Tell me more.'

'Can you keep it entirely secret? I mean, not tell anyone at all.'

I nodded and smiled. 'Yes, of course I can.'

'I have to meet someone in Ballater today. It's near Balmoral. He's expecting me.'

It sounded full of intrigue.

'Who?'

He smiled. And I noticed, for the first time, that John had his Sherlock Holmes deerstalker sitting on his lap. It seemed to take on some strange significance. 'There are some things that you must not ask.' He smiled wryly.

Suddenly Ted's voice crackled over the microphone and the music was turned low.

Anyone check whether 'the Royals' have arrived for their holidays?'

Dolly, sitting immediately ahead of me, said 'Yes. I looked yesterday. They are here now.'

'Good. We're only fifteen miles along the glen from them, so have your cameras handy.'

Across the coach there were excited murmurs.

Ted and Dorothy were behind Jill and I. And Dorothy leaned forward to ask how I was feeling.

'Well, OK, I guess. But it's good to be out on the road again. Now I know how a travelling circus might feel.'

At this she laughed and said 'fresh pastures.'

John was busy making notes from a tourist guide. Was he was trying to find out where he was meant to meet 'the mysterious stranger'.

Beside me Jill was enjoying the passing scenery.

There was not even a single car on the roads this morning. Skylarks hovered close to the fields and large golden eagles circled high overhead. Rabbits busy about their own business, foraged for food, and the young ones, almost like toys, jumped and played. Small rivulets seemed to glide effortlessly through the fields, glistening, shimmering, full of fish, while close to the water dragonflies darted on gossamer wings.

It was, a very Highland day; blustery, cool, breezy and with the scents of the fields blowing straight into your lungs. Such an enervating cocktail of goodness I had always encountered in the high mountains of Switzerland. I guessed it be to do with hills and altitude. It was both exhilarating and calming; all at the same time.

A sense of togetherness was with us in the coach. Everyone, apart from Charles was 'on board' as we took the road North to Royal Deeside. It was here in

1852   that Queen Victoria and her husband Albert, fell in love with  this part of Scotland and decided to buy an estate and build their own   Royal home, Balmoral Castle.

'The Royals' have loved it ever since. Jill had been reading all about it. She  said suddenly 'It's such a wonderful fairy story of how Queen Victoria and her husband, Prince Albert  came to stay here, isn't it.'

I nodded. 'We must make  sure we  tell Dolly all about it.  Queen Victoria was a great romantic.  But not too many people  know that side  of her.'

Suddenly Jill said 'Has John mentioned  anything more about  the diamonds?'

'He said the police   are checking  their authenticity today.'

The music was suddenly on again in the coach. And Ted asked if we would like to stop to  enjoy the view.

There was a general buzz  of excitement as  everyone said 'yes'

At the next  passing place he pulled the large coach into the side.  We  trooped out,   one  by  one,  into  the windswept 'wilderness' of far forests and   glens that swept  away into the distance and seemed to go on and on.

It felt good to be here, away from so much that seemed like a civilised life,  yet offered so little.

'I'm so glad that I came' said Jill suddenly, as though overcome with the emotion of  such  natural   grandeur around us.

Dorothy came over, with Don. He was taking cine film shots for a Scottish film he now planned. 'Smile please' said Dorothy with a twinkle in her eye. 'Come on Dolly, you're in this picture too. Anyone else?'

Two other ladies joined us as she snap-snapped.'That is fantastic' said Dorothy. 'You all look so happy and natural and the background is magnificent.'

Once back on the road again Ted was in fine form. He switched down the radio and started to tell us about the Speyside Malt Whisky Trail. All these whisky distilleries are in the River Spey area.

And we were passing them quite soon. 'Wish we had more time - and a night here - we could visit them. You'd like that. Full of great characters, a fantastic way to relax and learn at the same time. They show the whole process of making malt whisky.'

We were listening with interest.

'On the right is the River Dee. One of the finest salmon rivers in the world; that's where the Queen Mother used to fish.'

Suddenly Dr Craig said 'Are we stopping in Ballater, Ted?'

'Well, if it's not too busy I thought you'd like to see the little shops where the Queen sometimes looks in. Real visitor area. It gets a bit busy of course but maybe we'll be lucky.'

But then everything changed. We arrived to a battery of press photographers and a policeman flagged us down. Ted stopped and spoke to him, then laughed. 'Seems we're expected. The 'Bonnie Prince Charlie' Coach Tour is going on TV. We've a photocall across the street. All the press are here.'

Everyone looked a bit glum.

'The police have asked us to do it, to keep the pressure up on the thieves. Are we game?'

Thinking of Charles, we all said a reverberating 'yes.'

Suddenly John was ringing Charles on his mobile. But it did not connect.

'The mountains are blocking the signal' he said bleakly.

'What about your appointment?' I asked him furtively.

'I'll just slip away. Don't worry, I know exactly where I'm going. I'll be back in thirty minutes. But don't let Ted take the coach without me.' He smiled and touched my arm.

'Well, don't do a Charles. We haven't got him back yet.'

We both exchanged serious glances. And he nodded quietly. 'I know. I won't.'

The press were asking us about Charles. We knew little. And could only repeat what a nice guy he was.

'Is he a descendent of the true 'Bonnie Prince Charlie'? asked one girl journalist crisply.

'Yes - we certainly think so ' boomed a voice that

sounded like Hamish Craig's. Well he had been talking to Charles endlessly. They had spent evenings together at The Deerstalker. If anyone he would be the one likely to know.

'Who are we speaking to?' asked an attractive blonde reporter, looking straight at Hamish.

'Dr Hamish Craig. I'm a London GP and my special hobby is Scottish genealogy. I've written a book or two on the subject.'

'And you're a Scot?' asked one of the men of the press.

'Of course. Edinburgh born and bred.' He laughed quickly. 'On this occasion I'm here in the Highlands on holiday.'

That gave the press a good concrete line to work on. They could see we were no lightweight set up.

More pictures followed and Hamish was asked to give a TV interview. He spoke to them about Charles. Then they alighted on Dolly.

'Do you have any Scots ancestors?' asked a young red haired Scotsman.

'Yes, of course, I'm a MacGregor on my mother's side. I may be related to Rob Roy' said Dolly with pride.

This was history indeed.

Cameras clicked again and Dolly looked pleased and amazed. 'I was on the phone to New York only this morning telling my sister, Madge.'

'Do you know much about Rob Roy?' said a female

press voice, a little disparagingly.

'I'm learning. I gather he was 'pretty unusual' she laughed. 'And not always 'the good guy'.

Don and Dorothy Oldenshaw were cine filming and answering questions at the same time. As Don explained, he was filming it all for his own motion picture.

'Are you enjoying this 'adventure'? said the blonde reporter.

At that Jill piped up. 'If you mean, losing our Bonnie Prince Charlie then No! He's a great guy. He's like a son to us ladies. We're not leaving him behind when we leave Scotland.'

'And what of the Dechter diamonds, where are they?' asked a serious lone voice from the press.

'That's for the police to say' said Ted. 'Best contact them at Glenmorchie House. They are issuing a statement this very morning.'

'Now we would like to take a walk around Ballater, if you'll excuse us' said Ted, indicating by his tone that the press call was over.

We all started to move away, grateful to escape. Jill and I went into a small old fashioned stone fronted shop with a beautiful, ornate Royal warrant crest over its door.

We both picked postcards and then Jill chose a Caithness glass paperweight for herself and the most exquisite Scottish Celtic silver drop earrings for her sister, Mary, who it seemed had a birthday coming up soon.

Tiny bottles of Drambuie liqueur caught my eye.

The label read 'The drink of Prince Charles Edward Stuart.' A small leaflet in the tiny box explained that the liqueur was made from a mix of herbs and a dozen different malt whiskies; a secret recipe given by Prince Charles Edward Stuart to the Mackinnons of Strathaird on the Isle of Skye.

It was his personal thank you when the Mackinnons found him a safe boat that took him from Skye back to France in 1746 following his failed battle at Culloden.

Since then the Mackinnon family has kept the recipe a closely guarded secret. And today they market the liqueur worldwide.

'Lovely isn't it. I'll buy this for Charles' I said quietly. Jill nodded.

The lady in her 60's behind the counter, smiled gently and said 'You'll be from The Coach Trip, then?'

We nodded.

'I've been reading about that poor boy' she was glancing at the picture of Charles spread all over the papers on the display stand. 'A terrible business - but wish him well from me.'

'That was really lovely of her, wasn't it' I said to Jill as we walked into the open air.

I followed Jill across a small street to meet Dr Craig and the Oldenshaws and I could not get her kind comment out of my mind. Everyone was thinking about Charles.

We must get back and get him out, as soon as possible. What were we doing spending time looking for keepsakes in Ballater when Charles was in danger? And where, for goodness sake, was John?

# CHAPTER TWELVE

## *The 'Holmes' mystery deepens*

John was busy: keeping his mystery appointment.

After opening the small gate he had walked the length of the stone-flagged drive, deep in thought. The house beyond did not look welcoming.

It was unrelieved grey stone, yet a few summer flowers had tried to spring up and blossom on either side of the white painted door. And a rose bush with pink blossoms caught his eye. John was by no means a gardener. But such a sturdy bush would bloom year after year, with no attention from anyone.

There was the yap yap of a small dog as he approached. Gratefully it was on the inside.

John did not like small dogs; they were the biters. And he was in no mood for that sort of thing today.

As he knocked on the heavy door knocker, it opened at once.

No surprise. He knew he was expected.

The elderly man greeted him with a shuffle of the feet as he let him in.

'Mr Watson of the Sherlock Holmes Society, I ken.'

He was about 75 or 80. And slightly stooped. He had once been tall, but the bent shoulders took this away. And his hair was white; his face gaunt.

'Aye, get ye doun … ' he said to the dog. And the small Scots terrier vanished obligingly to sit under an upright chair. It was as though she was awaiting her master's next command.

'I'm sorry. We said about mid-day and I'm late' John started to explain.

'It does n'e matter.'

'Are you a member of the Holmes Society. Is that why you wanted to see me?' said John, feeling a little uncomfortable now.

'Nay. I'm one of the family.'

'..the family?'

'Aye. Sit ye down. And I'll explain.'

John had found himself a straight back chair in the small, neat room. And wondered what news he was now about to hear.

'I'm related to Conan Doyle, not by the blood, ye' ken' he paused a second. 'But by marriage. My dear wife, Annie, was his niece. She lived at 'the big hoose'.

John had at last started to understand his Scottish accent. 'Go on.'

'The big hoose, as ye' may have understood is Glenmorchie Hoose.'

'Ah' John listened carefully.

'Annie told me, when she was dying, that the

147

manuscript, the one ye' seek 'The Case of the Mysterious Monster' is at the big hoose.'

'She asked me not to tell the secret except to a real Sherlock Holmes disciple.'

'Conan Doyle gave it to Annie 'for safety, ye ken' and she had made a promise that it would remain locked safely away from his publishers and his family.'

'But why?' It sprang out and John almost wished it hadn't.

He paused. And thought about it.

'Conan Doyle was fed up with all the publicity about Sherlock Holmes. He had made enough money for his lifetime and Annie said that 'the Monster' book was too macabre even for him.'

'Even though he wrote it?' John's eyes widened.

The old man smiled. 'Aye, even though...'

John and the man whose name he still did not know, nor think to ask, were on the same wavelength.

'What would you like me to do?'

'Take it, man, take it. And promise me you'll give it to the Sherlock Holmes Society for their records. Not for publication mind ye'.

'Have you read it?'

He shook his head. 'Nay. No-one has.'

Then he reached into his waistcoat pocket and found a crumpled piece of paper which he started to unravel.

'You haven'a asked me where it is young man?'

'No. I haven't.'

'Here. I feel in my old bones I can trust ye'.        He handed John the piece of paper with a handsketched pencil drawing.

John  grasped it and looked in more detail, peering to see.

'It's in the library?'

'Aye. The big library at  Glenmorchie  Hoose. That's where my Annie put it, and left it  all those years ago. She made a promise.  Now you must do your best to keep it.'

'You mean, I've not to take money for it.'

'Aye..' He was unsmiling. 'There's a curse  if you do.'

John nearly dropped the  crumpled piece of paper.  And he heard the terrier  gently growl. It was like a warning.

'There's  a few people who would like to get their sticky fingers  on it.. I'll warn ye' He paused. 'Like  young Andy and his brother Ian.  They'll stop at nothing.'

John gasped.   'Andy, with the fair hair, who works at The Deerstalker in Edinburgh.'

The man nodded and looked tired. As though he had had enough of explaining.

'Let's have a 'wee dram' to seal the  deal.' He said with a slight hint of a  sparkle.  'I can see you're a serious man. Ye'll do your best, I know.  I can trust ye'.

He poured  two 'doubles', and  raised his glass. 'Come, man, dinna' be alarmed.  Ye'll not find it hard to get hold of the manuscript.'

He took back the note 'It's here.'

'Behind the other books?'

He nodded.

John knew he owed the man a lot and clinking his glass with his and trying to take the pure malt whisky down 'in one' but not managing, he was about to ask his name.

'Alistair McDonald. And here's my address. Just send me a wee note, when you've got it. Just to let me know, ye ken.'

'I'll send you more than that. I've been looking for this for years.' John gasped. 'It's the reason I came here to the Highlands.'

The old man ignored him.

'Aye, and a word of warning. Be careful with your young friend from Toronto. Get him out of the Royal apartment by tonight.'

Now John's look had changed to one of alarm.

'You know about that?'

'I watch TV and read the papers.'

'You mean he's in danger?'

'Aye. They'll stop at nothing to get the manuscript. Now on ye' go. Don't miss the coach.' He was already shuffling John to his front door.

'Thank you.' John wondered what more he could say.

The old man smiled. By now the wee dog was at his side and looking excited. She was even wagging her stubby tail. 'Just let me know.'

'Remember we drank on it and a Scotsman never goes back on his word when its sealed over a 'dram'. If ye're ever this way again - maybe next year - look in. Ye'll be more than welcome.'

'You're keen to let the Holmes Society have it?'

The old man paused, then turned, and took a picture off the wall. It was recognisably him, some thirty years before, being decorated by the Queen. Annie, his wife, was at his side.

'The MBE' he said proudly. 'I was a police detective. They said I was good.'

It was a poignant moment. The two men stood, looking at each other, lost in their past.

John had turned, waved once and walked away. Now he understood why Alastair McDonald had wanted him to call.

He would return to see him again.


By the time John had walked the small lane and reached the coach we were all safely inside. Ted was standing with one foot on the step, counting and checking his passengers.

'I was just wondering where you were' he quipped. 'Another two minutes and we'd have gone.'

Both men laughed as John jumped on board.

He settled into a seat beside Harry Sparrow and both men sank into comfortable silence. Ted closed the door and stepped into his driving seat.

'Well' he said 'Did anyone see the Queen?'

Two voices were beginning to call out 'No', when Ted interrupted. 'My goodness. Get your cameras, quick. Here comes a royal car.'

Like children directed to do something, we did.

A muddy Land Rover stopped outside a shop and in dashed the driver. No, it wasn't the Queen. But it looked remarkably like Prince Charles. He was in tweeds and hunting gear. What on earth was he doing in the village, I wondered, shopping?

Ted paused the coach. We were obviously going nowhere now. Two minutes later the driver re-appeared. Cameras clicked into action. It was HRH Prince Charles, the Queen's eldest son, heir to the throne of Britain. He looked trim and fit and as though he had just come off the moors. Or maybe his gear was normal 'off duty' wear for his relaxing Scottish holiday.

Everyone gasped. And as he turned he caught sight of the coach - and the faces within - and he looked up and half smiled.

'Well.' said Dolly excitedly. She was three seats ahead of me and bobbing up and down to get all the pictures that she could. The Oldenshaws were equally busy.

'Didn't I say we had a good chance of seeing 'the Royals' said Ted swinging the coach into action as the Land Rover with its driver and a male passenger, probably an aide or detective, drove away. 'Everyone leaves them alone up here, that's why the Royal family likes Deeside.'

I could hear Dolly and Dorothy exchanging animated conversation. We now had quite a few very happy tourists.

Just behind Ted John sat and looked unseeing at the hills and glens.

The countryside slipped by but his mind was on Glenmorchie and what he had to do next.

The warning about young Charles Edward rang in his mind. It clanged like a giant bell.

He had no doubt that Alastair McDonald was telling the truth. What he did not understand was how the manuscript figured in the business of Charles being taken captive. And were the same people behind the jewel robbery at the Deerstalker? Was it all connected?

If Andy was involved - and his brother Ian - then why?? He had to know this, to understand how best to trap the villain.

Alastair McDonald had said they had to get Charles out 'before tonight'.

He was still thinking about it all, when a flashing light in his brain started to signal. It could not be ignored. What was coming through was that Fiona McGill, the hospitable hostess and proprietor at The Deerstalker, was somehow involved in it all too.

John had shrugged. Why was his over-active brain

even thinking that? She wasn't a rogue. Or a jewel thief.   Indeed he felt rather sorry for her, if, as Ted said, she was  finding life hard following her husband's death.

Yet it seemed strange that Andy worked there. And within days was  also at the Glenmorchie.   And if Conan Doyle  kept masses of his manuscripts at the Deerstalker, why was it that one of the most sought after, The Case of the Mysterious Monster, should remain hidden at  Glenmorchie?

There was a link. But John could not think of it.

It was rather like playing a game of tennis, when every ball you hit  flew off at a tangent.

Before  going into a ten minute doze - something  he was famous for - at 'the Met' in the old days, John had had one other inspirational thought.

It was: MONEY.

Odd how easy it was  to  brush   relevant things aside when in fact you shouldn't. Eventually John fell  asleep. Most of the coach party was  almost asleep too.  It must have been the clear and relaxing Highland air.

We      awoke with a start as the coach pulled off the A93, and   Ted was saying    over the microphone. 'We're  nearly  home. Hold  onto  your  seat  belts everybody.  Now for the bumpy bit.'

It was only  4.30. And the day had settled to being gloriously sunny. Around us the mountains reached to a clear blue sky, and birds were singing from the   trees.

154

I saw the occasional  small rabbit out with its brothers and sisters, jumping and skipping about enjoying their day. Sheer heaven, I thought.

But what about Charles?

Ten minutes later when we stepped off the coach it was the first word on everyone's lips. Even without needing to say so aloud, we all knew we had to find our Bonnie Prince Charlie, as fast as we could.

Ted paused for a moment as he closed the coach door.

'John has suggested we meet up in the main lounge  in twenty minutes to plan our next move regarding Charles.'

John was beside him. Everyone nodded and said they would be there.

'Have you any more news?'  I asked John, as we stepped inside Glenmorchie.

'Well, Charles' father is arriving  tonight' he paused for a moment. 'My contact in Ballater said it was urgent for us to free Charles today.'

I nodded.

John was looking thoughtful 'We have to decide how to get to Charles. No more time to spare. I'll run the rest of the film again.  If it comes to a serious raid  through the house, well, we've more than enough people.' He added suddenly. 'I've just tried to call Charles on the mobile. He's not answering.' He looked worried.

I could hear the Scots voice of old Jock along the corridor. It had his distinctive accent, very raw,  though

whether   it was Glaswegian with a touch of Highland I
was not certain. It was raised slightly, as though some
kind of argument was going on. There was no sign of
the police.

As I walked towards my turret room, I realised that
suddenly the house seemed, though just as huge and
grand, rather a little less intimidating.

Maybe it was because we were about to mount an
onslought of our own. It was a counter attack   that
would set the glen reeling. And have the international
media enthralled for days.

But for the moment I  sat, and  then lay stretched out on
my bed  sipping a lemon drink  innocently wondering
what John was  planning.

I  changed into a  blue sports suit; track trousers and a
matching sweatshirt top and  flat comfy shoes.

As I walked down the staircase Jill met up with me.

She too had changed into sturdier clothes; blue jeans
and a polo neck jersey in red.   She looked superb.

'Hi' she said. 'I'm going to suggest at the meeting that
we all go through the house like, well, like vigilantes  ..
You know, knocking and pulling on every door, until
we do find the way to Charles' secret room.'

'We may have to do some damage like battering doors
down' I said.

'Yes, I know.  And  I'm all for that'   she said sounding
quite aggressive and adding 'Dolly entirely agrees and
so do most of the  rest.     We were talking on the way

156

back on the coach.'

'Good. Exactly what I thought too. We'll tell John and Ted at this meeting.'

In the lounge the film was already rolling. John had started it and was discussing the library where he still felt certain Charles had met his strange fate.

John and Ted were running the meeting.

And when someone said 'Can you tell us what's happening?' Ted stepped to the front.

'The police have come up with some vital clues while we've been away. They'll be back with us in about an hour to explain. But Charles is still missing.'

'As for the staff, Andy is no longer being held by the police. He may be here later today. If anyone should see him please let us know, without delay.'

He paused 'John and I would like to see that young man. We've a few serious questions for him.'

'I'd go so far to say that we think Andy is 'up to his neck in this'. Sadly the police are not so sure..'

Ted turned back to look at John. 'Now you take over John. You know more about it all than I do.'

John slipped into the central spot. The film still ran behind him.

'I spent some time in Ballater at lunchtime today with a man who knows the set up here. I don't want to alarm you. But we have to get Charles out as our first priority. Any ideas?'

At this Jill, who was sitting beside me, leapt up.

157

'A large number of us feel we should be  battering down doors in our search.'

John nodded.   This was serious stuff. He knew exactly how they felt.  'I agree.'

'The police won't like it.' said a man at the back.

There was a general roar of discontent, as though no one really cared what the police thought. If they couldn't rescue Charles, then we had to.

~ ~

At about the same time Charles Edward, who had lost all track of the days he had been kept prisoner, was feeling  a mixture of elation and depression.

Elation because from the huge book that he had been reading assiduously since his arrival in the boudoir had come  a truly startling piece of  corroboration  of his claim to be a descendant  of the royal house of Stuart.

It was a tiny paragraph  that merely said that  Charles Edward Stuart had a  distinctive mole high on his left shoulder blade  above the arm, on his back.  And that his father had this, plus his daughter by  Clementina Walkinshaw, Charlotte.

Charles knew he had this too.

Could it be that such  birthmarks, if this is what they were,  were handed down over the generations. It was an amazing and almost unbelievable thought.

However  his elation was quickly  dampened  by  the

thought that, unless help arrived soon, it would all be of no consequence.

He had finished the food and drinks in the hamper. The room was becoming stuffy, indeed grotesque. He had found a small side cabinet that was a bidet. And had had to use it.

How long had he been here alone and without a call from John?

He tried to use his phone. But there was no signal at all. The battery had long ago given out.

Charles lay on the bed deciding on his next course of action. It was no use waiting. He felt that he must do something now!

He stood up and walked around the room. There had to be a way out. He wondered how on earth the hamper had arrived. Probably by a chute; the kind that often large houses and hotels have for laundry and - he smiled grimly - for the rubbish..

It hardly fitted in with his claim to be Bonnie Prince Charlie's descendant, he thought ruefully. But he felt sure that Bonnie Prince Charlie, who had known serious deprivation while escaping from the wrath of the English following Culloden, would have well understood.

If he could find the rubbish chute, he would be saved.

Carefully, sometimes on his knees, in the dark of just a flickering candle - his last candle, unless he found more tucked away - Charles continued his search among the drapes and the woodwork seeking his exit.

~ ~

Outside, much was happening.

The coach party, every single one of them, were on the hunt.

In the now cool sunshine we borrowed garden tools from an old stable, plus a pitchfork, a hayrake, and even a mallet: armed to the hilt we proceeded in three's around Glenmorchie, trying to locate its cellars, exits and any 'odd corners', as John had put it.

Harry Sparrow, his wife Ivy, and Dr Craig were one party. I teamed up with the Oldenshaws. And Dolly, Jill and Mr Jenkins were to do the front of the house.

The rest of the party divided themselves up into three's and four's and we set off.

Ted and John, armed with spades, took one side of the house each, to oversee the operation and John said, it would be like police combing an area, for clues.

'What should we look for?' I asked, as I set off.

'Anything, anything you think unusual and of course any entrances, like concealed cellars.'

There should be lots, I thought to myself. Old houses, even quite small old houses always had masses of disused cellars and outhouses, usually half underground. This huge house had to be full of them, with such a long, long history.

It was Ivy Sparrow who thought to look in a large square rubbish bin.

She pulled out a black bag, tied at the top with string. She was curious because, as she said later, it had very little in it. Usually black bags are full to the top when thrown into the bin for disposal.

A tiny, quiet little lady in her 40's, she was now the centre of attention. She handed her 'find' to Ted. It was, wrapped in heavy white plastic, bound together with a white rubber band. And quite obviously not rubbish. But a proper parcel. It carried no label or address.

Ted shook it carefully. And paused a moment.

'I'll show it to John before we have a closer look.' he said going to find John.

Meanwhile we all continued looking for an entrance or exit.

Dolly, working with a heavy garden fork, which she said reminded her of childhood days on their farm in California, found a cellar exit and we got Ted to look closer into it once she had taken the earth away.

'I am sure there will be a way out of the house through one of these exits.' said Dolly.

From the front of the house there was suddenly much excitement.

Mr Jenkins thought he heard a slow tap - tapping noise. Sure enough, when we all arrived we heard it too.

John bent down with Mr Jenkins and with the mallet

gave a sharp tap-tap back. There was silence for a moment as we all held our breath.

We were all standing there concentrating like mad, waiting and listening, when with a sudden rush and a roar of engines and squeal of brakes fast coming to a halt, the front of the house descended into chaos.

We turned round to see two police cars, plus the long white van and another black car that looked like a new Rover, all with people getting out of them.

I was acutely aware that Ted had the parcel from the rubbish bin. But luckily he had already tucked it into his inside coat pocket. John looked across at Ted and smiled.

'Everything allright?' said a young voice. It was fair haired Andy striding towards us.

'Well, we were just taking a look around the place' said Harry Sparrow, quite ignoring the fact that we must have looked the strangest collection of people, armed as we were, each with an implement.

At that stage John stepped forward.

'I'd quite like to have a chat when you've a moment, is it Andy?"

The young man, smartly dressed in a black suit that looked more right for the city than any Highland estate, let a flash of doubt cloud his face. Then brightly he lit up with a grin.

'Yes, of course. I'll see you in the house before dinner.'

We all stood on one foot and the other waiting for the people from the cars to go. But they hung about. Andy walked into Glenmorchie with two other young men of about his own age.

The police went in quite separately. And John remarked that he did not recognise any of them as those he had seen earlier in the day.

'Shall we ask one of them about Charles?' I said quietly to John.

'Yes, what are they doing?' said Jill, beside me.

'Let's not be too hasty' said John suddenly. 'I think we are seeing more than we realise.'

'Shall we carry on?' ventured Mr Jenkins, obviously disappointed that we had been interrupted at the vital moment.

Ted and John walked over. John leaned down, while everyone kept watch as though by spoken command. He tapped with the mallet, once, twice, three times.

We waited … and then heard a sharp, but feint tap, tap, tap.

Someone was responding. We all looked as though we wanted to cheer. But dared not do so, in case Andy and the others heard. And came to see what was going on.

'I never could remember my morse' said John.

'I doubt if Charles will know it' added Dr Craig. 'I have a little though, here, let me try SOS. Learned it in the cadets.'

He knocked out a few sounds.

And the feint tap, tapping was returned.

We all sighed and smiled. It was Charles. And he was somewhere under the house at the front, near enough to hear us. All we had to do was find a way in. There were tears in my eyes. And I could see Dolly and Jill and Dorothy Oldenshaw, all looking damp eyed too.

'Right' said John, putting his mallet on the ground. We have found Charles. We can get him out - but we will need to batter our way in.'

Three hours to darkness. Could we wait until then?

John called another 'war council'. And suggested that in daylight we would quickly be spotted. At night we could put on all sorts of distractions - noisy ones like a ceilidh - to help prevent anyone being any the wiser.

We would ask Jock to play the pipes 'nice and loud' and do some of the reels we learned at The Deerstalker. As we all relaxed with a whisky mac held in our still sore, and grubby, hands we discussed the details.

The noise sounded brilliant cover. Even though Dolly groaned a little. 'Is there no other music here?'

'Yes, but bagpipes are so noisy' I started to explain. 'And everyone concentrates on them.' My eyes were trying to tell her why we really needed the bagpipes tonight.

It was arranged for 10pm. Jock, when we found him, was delighted 'ta be asked'.

Now we had to find some tartan and Highland gear to look the part. We would have one incredible party !

# CHAPTER THIRTEEN

## *Highland rescue*

Glenmorchie  House glowed pink and gold in the evening sunset; the light dipping down behind stark mountains that looked black in outline.

Suddenly, as though by magic, like a theatre curtain, the night clouds swiftly descended and within minutes it was dark.

Inside, everyone was busily watching the news on television.

A brief clip of Charles' father, a rather handsome and tall 55 year old Canadian, led the Scottish news. He was at Prestwick airport, near Glasgow. And on his way.

Jill said suddenly 'He's rather  dashing.'

'I hope we've  rescued Charles before he arrives' I said 'Or I think he will be a very angry man.'

The news mentioned the police and that they had  'a suspect'. And that the missing jewels  were now in the hands of the police.

'Oh, I guess that's  Dolly handing in the jewels this morning' said Jill quickly.  'Seems like ages ago. I wonder if they've told her  if she'll get the reward.'

'I certainly hope so.'

'There's something I want to tell you' said Jill quietly.
'Promise me you won't faint.'

'Course I won't. I don't make a habit of it' I laughed.

But what she told me was quite scary. And spine chilling.

'When I came back from putting the spades away in the stables, guess what I saw?'

I looked, keeping quiet and inviting her to continue.

'Really strange, large    triangle footprints, about eight inches across.'

I must have looked curious more than terrified. So she grabbed me by the arm. 'Come and have a look. It's not far.'

What we saw was an imprint, a huge animal imprint of a triangle foot,  with clawmarks.  In the rough cart track it was very definite.

'What do you think it is?' she said almost brightly.

'Maybe someone is trying to frighten us. It could be as simple as that.    I really think they want us to go.'


John had that distinct feeling too. Only he was back in the library, with Alastair  McDonald's plan in his hand.

He had had no time until now.  But he wanted to find the Conan Doyle manuscript, if only to keep his promise to the old Scot. Tonight might be his only chance.

John searched, lifting books  off  the shelves and

running his fingers behind. When there was nothing, he carefully put the books back.

After fifteen minutes he realised it was not exactly where Alastair had said it would be. This could take hours; hours that he did not have.

John was engrossed in his search and did not hear the door open. He was not aware of being watched until suddenly he felt another presence. John half jumped as he looked round and caught sight of Andy.

'Looking for something?' said the young man.

John half smiled.

'Well, just a book.' He felt distinctly guilty.

'But a particular book.'

'Yes. You could say that.'

John remembered that he wanted to see this young man and decided to turn the tables and ask him a few questions.

'We had a meeting. Is this the right time to ask you one or two things?'

'As good a time as any' said Andy

He was unprepared for John's curiosity.

What part do you play in this hotel. I mean, are you 'family' or a 'manager?'

Andy did not answer. He stood back looking straight at John, and almost truculent.

'I want to know why my friend Charles is imprisoned here?'

'I think that's the wrong question John Watson, former

Chief of CID at the Met. I think the question should be 'what can I do to get Charles out?' You're not a CID officer now.'

'Even being a leading light in the Sherlock Holmes Society doesn't excite me either. But that's why you're here.'

John kept his cool, though with difficulty.

'I'm a paying guest at this hotel. My only desire is to see Charles safely back on the tour, to continue his holiday.'

Andy thought for a moment.

John decided that on appearances he wasn't very bright. He had to stop and think about everything. No speed of mind at all.

'But why are you here in this library? Not looking for a book, but I believe a Conan Doyle manuscript.'

John hesitated.

'I was told it might be here. True, I'd like to glance through it before I leave. 'Holmes' is a hobby. This is one work I have not yet seen.' He felt he would press the advantage, adding. 'Is it here. Or am I wasting my time?'

Andy paced the room. Then turned. 'Yes, it is. I have it.' He paused waiting for the effect it would have on John. And when he saw little facial show of the man's emotion, he continued. 'Do you want it, Mr Watson?'

'I'm not sure' said John, putting the remaining books

away. 'Anyway you are probably lying in your teeth.'

'But you don't know for sure'

'The book doesn't belong to you..' started John.

'So. You've been talking to Alastair.' Andy smiled and was about to leave the room. 'The manuscript is not his to give away either. And as everyone knows possession is nine tenths of the law.'

He smiled before leaving.

'You'll be safely gone by the morning Mr Watson. I'll let you have the manuscript, and I'll tell you, for a collector it's a beauty. I'll let you have it, if you find me the diamonds and sapphires.'

'The police already have them. You're a bit behind with that news.'

'That's where you're wrong. The one's handed in this morning by your American lady were not the real diamonds. But a very good likeness. The real gems are still missing. They have completely vanished. And they are now valued at well over £250,000.'

'And Charles, what about Charles?'

Andy half grinned. 'Well, he's worth £100,000 I would think. But maybe his father will fork out for him. I think so.'

Suddenly it was all becoming clear.

'So it's money you're after !'

Andy still waited at the closed door. And before leaving he said. 'I know you won't believe me; detectives always see things as black or white, villains or innocents.   All I can say is I am not a villain.

'But yes, I need to raise money,  a vast sum, one way or the other'.

'What you are doing to Charles is pure villainry' John spluttered 'Don't deceive yourself.'

'You won't believe me.  But we haven't done anything to Charles.  He did it somehow all by himself.   I sent him the hamper so that he was at least, comfortable.

'The secret room really is 'a secret'. Even I do not know the entrance.'

'You must get him out.'

'We will.  Meanwhile it makes a very good story' he smiled.

'I'll no doubt see you later at the party.  My uncle Jock tells me he has been invited to play the bagpipes tonight.'

He left through the door then popped back in again. 'Oh, by the way. You really are wasting your precious time hunting for The Case of the Mysterious Monster. It's a pity that we did not  have this chat earlier.

'And  don't tell your friends all about our conversation. Some things are best discussed between only two people. Police officers normally understand that.'

'You're a police officer?'

'I was' said Andy, and left.

John sat down on one of the large  wooden carved back chairs. He did not yet know why Andy needed so much money.  Nor exactly who he was.   But  he felt that the young man was probably telling the truth. And his own experience as a police detective meant that he could believe that the smartly dressed, upright youngster had in fact been in the force too.

But more pressing now was to try to find the real diamonds. His mind switched to those that Ted was holding in his inside jacket pocket.

Swiftly he jumped up and put the last books back on the shelves.

He had to rely on Andy telling him the truth about the manuscript. Anyway he knew it was technically 'out of bounds' for him to be searching someone else's library in the hope of what? Stealing, or 'borrowing' the priceless item. If it was a family feud, he would have to deal with Andy now that he had been caught red-handed.

Quietly he left the room.

~ ~

Downstairs it was not yet 9pm. No bagpipes echoed. The whole house was resting. The ladies were trying to find tartan to wear tonight to capture the feel of the Highlands.

Once in his room John smiled.

He took a bottle of malt whisky from his sideboard, found a glass and poured out a wee dram. Then he added two 'fingers' of water. He drank it down and felt immediately better. And stretched out on his bed. Then he saw the note slipped under his door. It said simply "We have found vampire footprints in the drive. Hope you are OK" Jill and Amy.

John smiled and feeling he could hardly take this seriously, fell sound asleep.


In Jill's room we were busy swopping ideas about our 'party' clothes; Jill, Dorothy and myself.

Ted had loaned us his long length of Anderson tartan, with its hues of blue and red, and the grouse foot, which, though it looks quite macabre he said was 'traditional', and the Scottish way to secure the simple length of fabric.

You swing the fabric over one shoulder and it floats and twirls its own length, usually down to the knees. Over either trousers or a skirt its looks good. It needed no stitching; quite a boon as we discovered none us had any emergency needles with us.

Dorothy had her tartan trews from the States. And dashed off; changed into them and was back in minutes. We pinned the fabric over her shoulder with the claw; the beautiful fabric swung on either side. Wonderful. She 'twirled'. Both slim and trim, she laughed with delight.

'Now you are ready to go to the ball, Cinders' said Jill. We all burst into fits of giggles. It was all silly and very good fun.

There was a  quick knock on the door. Jill dashed to answer and it was Ted, with a big smile handing in some more tartan that he had  located.

'Ooh, thank you.'    Jill  turned.  'Look.' She held up armfuls of tartan fabric; one that I later learned was the famous Black Watch, dramatic in dark green, black and with a bright line of red; and the second a Royal Stuart, mainly in bold bright reds.

'This is the  Stuart clan, Bonnie Prince Charlie's'  she said, her smile now fading as we all thought of our young  friend.

'We're doing this, not really to  enjoy a party remember. We're  putting on this  party  to  try to rescue him. I'll wear the Royal Stuart, if I may.'

She brightened up and quickly tossed it to me.

'Now we need to find  either claw brooches …'

'Or safety pins' said Jill matter-of-factly, back to her old self again.

There was a great air of excitement.

We knew that  while  we danced the night away, with old Jock skirling the pipes,  Ted, John, Dr Craig, Don Oldenshaw, Harry Sparrow, Mr Jenkins and  in fact all the men on the coach  would use the  'cover' of such activity and noise  to hammer their way in to rescue Charles.

After our  dressing up session we all  made our  plans to meet  just before  10pm, when the party was to begin.

'I'm going to try to have a nap. I think we have a hectic night ahead' I said to Dorothy and Jill. 'What about you?'

They agreed.

'I've never been so exhausted. Still, I guess the music will perk us up.'

'And the whisky' laughed Dorothy.

'Plus there's a lovely buffet I gather. We haven't eaten much today.'

We went our separate ways.

I lay on my bed with the evening sunlight shining through the windows and  listened to the birds twittering, almost as though they were winding down for the day. They were pleasantly relaxed.

But trying  to nod off for an hour proved almost impossible. Thoughts of poor Charles and what he was going through ran around my brain.

Eventually I  switched on the radio  and  picked up on a programme all about  music in the 21$^{st}$ Century, and its leading  performers.  It  circled around Europe as well as  the UK. I was fascinated. And finally dropped off listening to  the soothing sound of  violin  strings and the 'cello being played in Paris.

When we  met up at just after ten,  the pipes were already echoing  through the  big house.

We walked down the main staircase. I glanced up at the huge  painting of Bonnie Prince Charlie  and  was disappointed to  note that it did not wink.

'You were dreaming, the other night' said Jill, eyeing me sideways.

'Oh that' I said, feeling acutely embarrassed.

We stepped into the banqueting hall like a Scottish trio; Jock stood at one end piping a loud and exciting tune. No-one seemed to be noticing. Dolly and some of the other ladies and men from the coach were at the buffet, debating what to eat. And picking and choosing.

When they saw us they all looked admiringly.

'You look stunning' said Dolly.

The huge long table fairly groaned under the volume of food. It was a table with massive round, oak, bulbous legs at intervals of every six feet; the heaviest table I had ever seen; built I suspected for events such as this.

The kitchen staff, now all on duty again, had excelled. From salmon in aspic jelly to roast venison, grouse, cold roast beef and fresh salads and hot baked potatoes, there was everything to enjoy. Even cock-a-leekie soup for those of us wanting to try another real Scottish soup. It was no formal sit down meal. But a superb buffet, with a sweet table that included gateaux, chocolate cake, glace bombe, fresh fruit and cheeses of at least twenty different varieties, from cheddar to stilton, gruyere and brie.

The coffee was not yet perking. But there waiting. And both wine and whisky were available.

'What a spread.' said Dorothy. 'It's just like Thanksgiving Night in the States.'

Dolly turned and agreed with her. 'Scottish food is very good. I just love it.' She was enjoying a plate of salmon with fresh salad and trimmings.

I heaved a sigh and turned to Jill. 'I've put on weight on this tour. Tonight I need to dance it off.'

Jill was the sort of person who remained as slim as a beanpole, even though she seemed to eat just as much as I did.

From the kitchen, two girls in white aprons over black dresses and wearing white caps appeared. They cut through straight to the dance floor. And began to take part in the reel. They were slim, light of foot and very fast. They then moved off the dance floor to steer other people on to start us all dancing.

Soon we were weaving in and out, learning this new Highland dance, everyone joining in.

I wondered how John and Ted were getting on outside. And if they had started their excavations. Two dances later we were suddenly aware of a crowd of people arriving. They were all young and wearing dinner suits and the girls were in beautiful long gowns. They chattered excitedly.

Jock knew them and indicated a warm welcome with a wave and a grin.

They stepped forward to help themselves to drinks, then prompted by the lively music decided to step onto the dance floor.

'I've been told they're from a nearby wedding party'

said Jill in my ear.

At the next  dance I sat out, mainly to gather breath. Dolly was alongside.

'Any news yet from 'the boys'?' I asked.

'They're outside working now.'

'I suppose the more the merrier' I added, looking at the young people all enjoying themselves.  They seemed to know the steps perfectly.

The young waitresses,  having played their part, left the floor and returned to the kitchen.

'It will keep Jock busy playing for this crowd' said Jill.

Then suddenly I turned.  Coming into the hall was Jenny, the receptionist. She  was  wearing a long  blue ball gown with a sash of tartan tied over it and had her hair swept up.  She looked stunning. And moved towards us.  To my astonishment she was wearing a diamond and  sapphire  necklace and matching drop earrings.  The Dechter diamonds, I  went to say aloud, then stopped myself. Or were they yet another set of fake diamonds?

She was with a man in a kilt and full Highland  evening dress.  They moved on to the dance floor. It was obvious she didn't care who knew  or saw the jewels. Everyone was looking at her.  She was flaunting them.

I nudged Jill  who put her hand to her mouth and let out a gasp.

'Do you think we should tell Ted or John?'

'I don't know, obviously  its   no secret or she wouldn't

be wearing them. Remember, Ted said there were two sets of fakes.'

Jill excused herself saying she was off to the ladies room. But I suspected that she was also off to see John and Ted. At least I hoped so.

Five minutes later she was back.

'I've had a word with John. He says it's three foot thick concrete and they can't seem to make any impression.'

'Is everyone there?'

She nodded. 'Yes, all the men are helping and trying to work out what to do next. It might mean bringing in an excavator but there's no chance of that this time of night.'

She stopped for a second.

'Have they contacted Charles?'

'They sent a signal, and he replied. They seem to think he can hear the loud music too.'

Jock was taking a break now. And a dozen of the young people came over to where we were sitting.

'Nice party' said a pretty girl.

'Are you on holiday here?'

She laughed. 'Well, yes and no. We're the actors from the film that was made here 'The Vampire of Glas Shiel'. Two of the actors got married today and we've been at their wedding. We thought we'd just drop by and visit the old place again and you have this fabulous party on. We're really thrilled.'

'You'll know Gloria…?' I started.

'Yes, of course.    She may drive over later, I certainly hope so.'  She laughed. 'We left her celebrating.    Do you know her?'

I told how we had been staying at The Deerstalker in Edinburgh on the night of the film's Scottish premiere. And that Gloria had popped in, looking fantastic.

'So you know all about the missing jewels?'

'Well, we were there  when they went missing, and the police arrived.   But we're on holiday really, a coach tour.'

A young man, now standing beside the girl, was listening and joined in.

'You're  The Coach Trip,  with Bonnie Prince Charlie. I've been reading all about it in the papers.' He extended a slim,  warm hand. 'Hello.'

A small crowd had gathered to listen and Dolly was now by my side.

'Is he allright,  the young man?' said the girl.

'Well, we hope so. But he's still in the secret room.'

'Oh God, no!'

Suddenly the young man turned and called across the room. 'Hey Jules. Hey, come over here.'

A pale  youngster, with blue eyes, and no more than twenty one,  slid over as fast as a breeze.

'Jules, you can help us, I know. Tell these ladies  what you found out about Glenmorchie when you were here making the film.'

The young man turned back to us.

'Jules knows the secret room. He can probably be a great help.'

'Is that where  Bonnie Prince Charlie is?'

'Yes, we think so' said Jill and I together.

Maybe this was the very breakthrough that we needed.

'Come with me' said Jules. He grabbed me with one hand  and Jill with the other and led  us towards a side room. We went up a staircase, through another room and then down a long spiral staircase that was almost too small for all three of us.

At the foot  was a small door with a large black iron sliding bolt on it. Jules stopped  and said 'I discovered it when we were setting up shots for the film. It was quite by chance. It leads into the secret room, the royal boudoir.'

Squeezed in as we were it was hard to  get the old bolt to move. Though  Jules tried and tried again and again.

'Can I tap a message to see if Charles is there?' I asked.

'Yes, of course.'

But  there was no  need to.

'Is that you Amy?'    said a voice.

It was Charles!

'Yes, yes.  We're all here' I gasped, half crying, half laughing with sheer excitement.

'Now, we need help.' I turned and as we started to rush back up the staircase Jules said in a very serious voice 'Keep together.  This is a very dangerous place.'

What did he mean, I wondered.

But that could wait.

'We're getting more help. Hang on Charles' I shouted out as loud as I could.

Outside John and Ted and 'the gang' were in the process of giving up for the night when we appeared with Jules.

Breathless, Jill and I started to explain.

'Jules knows the entrance into the secret room. We need a heavy mallet and a spade. Follow us.'

None of it was making sense. But that didn't matter.

John and Ted and all the others looked startled. Then John grabbed a spade and Ted picked up a mallet.

'Right, show the way' said Ted.

'There's almost no room to get down. We'll stay here. You go on with Jules.'

No-one hesitated.

Within minutes the three men were going through the small room and up the first staircase. We left them and waited.

In the distance as well as the sound of the bagpipes I could hear now the banging of Ted's mallet, pushing the long rusted bolt in its shaft to open the heavy studded door and set Charles free.

It seemed like an eternity. Yet it wasn't.

There was the excitement of voices and then Charles' unmistakable Canadian accent.

We looked at each other, Jill and I, too scared to speak.

'I think I'm going to cry' I said suddenly. 'I don't know why.'

And Jill was ahead of me, the tears streaming down her face.

Charles appeared like a knight from battle. He looked dishevelled and tired and his face had slimmed down.

'Thank you' he said, scooping us both up in his arms.

# CHAPTER FOURTEEN

## *Three extra on board*

It was a wonderful night. A night to dream about, read about but never to live through. It was too good, almost. I felt that I was in the middle of a strange, enchanting fairy tale.

Pinch me, and I would awaken to find it was all only a dream.

Yet when I looked across the crowded banqueting hall, with Jock the canny old piper, Dorothy and Jill dancing Highland reels, their tartan swirling, and young Charles, fresh, clean now, and changed into a suit and smiling broadly again, then I knew that it was all indeed reality.

John stood beside me on the right and Ted was just across by the banqueting table, tucking into his favourite venison while he listened to one of the engaging young actors.

These were suddenly all my new friends. It was odd to think that just over a week ago I knew none of them.

'A penny for your thoughts.'

It was John reading my mind.

'I was just wondering  if it was really all happening, it feels so strange.'

He smiled, put down his drink and then took mine.

'Come on, let's dance.'   And  he swept  us into a variation of the quickstep.    When we were dancing he said 'I know what you mean, Amy.'

'How could we have imagined this?' I said, smiling.

'And it's not quite finished yet.'

The party was certainly a great celebration.  Everyone was enjoying it. After the worry of the past two days, it was the moment to relax, enjoy a drink and share  each other's company.

'You know that Jules  is from the film company that made 'The Vampire' I started to say to Ted and John as we all enjoyed  some delicious  gateaux. 'That's how he knew where to find the secret room.'

They both nodded.

'Remember Gloria?'

'The film star?'

'Yes. She's coming here tonight.'  I heard a buzz  of noise and looked round.

And there she was; her red hair  swept up into curls on top of her head.  She looked very beautiful and wore a long  green gown, slimly cut and matching high  heels. Following the wedding she had been, it seems, into Inverness for the film's  Highland premiere.

Almost immediately she was introduced by one of the actors to Charles.

After some animated conversation they were being led onto the dance floor to take part in another Highland dance.

'Well' said Jill. 'That looks interesting. Bonnie Prince Charlie and the actress.'

'Now stop it. You're jumping to conclusions rather early' I said, smiling.

'Am I? They make such a gorgeous couple. You know she's American with Scottish ancestors. They have masses in common.'

Then Dolly was beside us. 'Did you see Gloria's jewels?'

I had been so taken looking at her red hair that it hadn't clicked. She too was wearing the complete set, necklet and earrings, of Dechter diamonds. Were they fakes too?

John appeared.

'Do you know, Jenny and Gloria are both wearing the missing jewels'

He almost dropped his glass.

'By the way' said John, 'Charles' father has arrived. They've put him in a room next to his son. He'll be down in a minute or two.' Then he vanished immediately to look, I thought, for Ted.

We were all keen to meet the man whom we had so far only caught glimpses of on television.

When Charles Edward senior stepped into the room with a beaming Ted and John on either side, the music

185

stopped. And then as Charles realised exactly who it was, and smiling broadly walked over, everyone started to cheer loudly and clap.

Jill and I looked at each other. This big handsome man, who now beamed and waved back, looked rather more than a little  surprised, almost as though  he was thinking: Have you laid this party on for me?

'Well?' I said to Jill.

Father and son were  embracing, talking and laughing and Ted and John were joining in this happy welcome.

'Later I'll ask Charles' father  for a dance' she said  with an intriguing  look.

Now, who's being 'forward'?

She smiled.

The party went on  like a breeze.  It seemed as though everyone was  dancing  away the problems of the past few days.  Charles was with us; unexpectedly his father was too.  And as for the diamonds?

Well, that was  for more knowledgeable people than  us to decide.

~ ~

In the morning, predictably, everyone had a hangover!

We were all tired; in fact totally exhausted.

It  had been a wild and merry night.   Full of emotion and energy.

On the car park  the  cars  from  the  actors  who had

186

decided to 'stay over' having had far too much to safely drink and drive, were littered like unrequired debris. The house was quiet. The morning papers lay on the huge mat, their headlines amazing and diverse. And some with pictures of Charles senior, snapped at Prestwick.

Was it only yesterday? So much had happened since.

It was ten o'clock before any guests began to stir.

The press rang Glenmorchie at about ten am. And Scottish TV followed with a news reporter wanting to do a mid-day story.

A young waitress told them the news they were all clamouring for.

'Bonnie Prince Charlie is free.'

It was enough. They took the scoop and flashed it around the world, or so it seemed. Then the phones all started to ring!

Was everyone interested in our small adventure?

Well, it seemed so.

Probably it had caught the imagination of a bored and too organised world; to hear of Bonnie Prince Charlie being held prisoner in 2001, was at least romantic and amazing.

And now he was free, so he could be interviewed. Photo opportunities, stories and tales to be told.

Earlier when I rang Jill from the slumbering luxury of my bed, I did not want to get up. Gosh, I was tired. My feet hurt. I had danced them sore!

She answered sleepily with a small voice.

'Hi. What day is it?'

That raised a small laugh. 'Major question. I don't know until I check it out.'

We burst into convulsive fits of giggles.

'I'd like breakfast in my room please..' I started.

More giggles.

We agreed to 'get ourselves together' and meet in half an hour in the hall and go downstairs.

We were not the only sleepyheads.

Downstairs the coffee was perking beautifully sending an aroma that was pure heaven throughout the whole lower floor.

We took large white pottery cups and poured black coffee. I helped myself to a large brown spoonful of sugar and stirred. This was bliss.

'No one much about. Don't say we're the first down.'

Jill nodded, enjoying her coffee too.

'What a fantastic night' she said suddenly.

'Unbelievable' I grinned.

My mind switching into gear I said suddenly 'We must ask Ted about the package that Ivy found in the rubbish bin.'

'It's probably still in his pocket' she murmured. 'After all yesterday's events.'

Jill walked over and picked up some of the papers. And we read them, just skimming.

'Do you know, I don't think I've ever had a hangover

but I'm feeling fragile today'.

'The soles of my feet are sore' I said, with a half smile.

'All that dancing.'

'Still, good for my figure. I've probably trimmed off a few pounds.'

'Are we going back to Edinburgh, today?'

'No idea' I said, helping myself to another black coffee and re-filling Jill's cup too.

Outside the day was warm, sunny and windy. A ten minute walk would be good for our lungs, we decided. And we took ourselves across beyond the stables into a field where a small stream gurgled and buttercups and daisies blossomed along with many flowers that were new to me, some with small yellow blossoms, others with tiny purple little 'faces'.

When Ted appeared at about mid-day, he too came out into the sunshine. He asked if we had slept well.

'That was a true Highland ceilidh' he said pausing to grin. 'One of the best I've ever been to.'

We looked slightly bemused.

'The best ceilidh's are practically impromptu, a bit like last night. We all had something to celebrate and we were there at the right time and ready to relax and enjoy ourselves.'

We were listening intently.

It seemed true of events in our own lives. Parties often clicked in this way, yet we had no name for them.

'One of the great things about the Scots from way back

189

is their ability to  have a wee dram, and  celebrate'
added Ted. 'They forget their cares until the next day.'
His final remark brought  us all back to earth.

Jill laughed. 'And here we are, wondering  which
diamonds are real and  how many sets of fakes there can
be, after  last night.'

'Well,  yes' said Ted thoughtfully.   'John and I had an
interesting  wee chat about that   at the height of the
ceilidh.  I wonder if he can remember a word of it.'

John was walking towards us.

We all four  paced gently up and down, enjoying the
fresh, fresh air and the freedom of  not being overhead,
except possibly by the birds.

John looked very fit and totally in 'Holmes' mode. He
even had a small book with him. Well, at least one of us
seemed in the mood for work.

'Did you enjoy last night?' I  asked.

Jill and I were eager to know.

He grinned. 'Yes.  Very much.  And I slept like a log.
Pretty fantastic night all round.'

'And the diamonds?'   said  Ted.

'Let's go inside and look at  the detail again. I saw you
out here  and came straight out. I'm dying for  a coffee
to tell you the truth.'

We all  followed John inside. And  Jill and I opted for
orange juices while the men had coffees.

John was in pensive mood. And had a question for Ted.

 'I wondered if we could  go to Aberdeen today,   and

190

return to Edinburgh tomorrow? It would give Charles the chance to see the glen and enjoy some Scottish scenery, and I have something I would like to do in Aberdeen'

John waited for Ted's response.

We were all listening and wondering.

'Well, we are so 'off schedule' on the tour that I reckon we can spare a day to do whatever we want.'

'It's to have the other diamonds valued' started John. He leant towards us, as he heard other voices in the hall. None of us said a further word. We waited for John to continue.

'Remember the package in the rubbish bin?' He needed to say no more. We had guessed. They were diamonds too.

'How many sets of fakes are there?' asked Jill, brushing a stray piece of hair from her forehead.

John raised both eyebrows.

'Well, I don't know. Jules was explaining last night that the film company had several made so that they could use them in the production. The original diamonds were considered too valuable and too easily lost, to be on the set.'

We smiled.

'So both Jenny and Gloria both could have been wearing false sets of diamonds' said Jill.

John took a small sip of coffee and stirred his cup.

'Yes.'

'I need to get this set valued. They look good, but the fakes are brilliant and I admit, I'm out of my depth.'

He went on 'There's a very good jeweller in Aberdeen just off the main street, Union Street, who will know if they are real.'

It seemed that John, in his inimitable fashion, had organised it all.

At lunch time, when most of the coach party were appearing, Ted called a meeting. 'We're thinking of heading into Aberdeen this afternoon. And back to Edinburgh tomorrow, everyone game?"

There was a resounding 'Yes!'

After hasty coffees and snacks, we set off. When we pulled away along the bumpy road, we had not one, but three extra passengers on board, Charles' father, whom we soon learned liked being called Edward, Jules and the stunning Gloria.

We turned onto the A93. John was seated beside me. Charles Edward next to Gloria. And Jill seated beside Edward. Jules was at the top of the coach chatting to Dolly. It seemed he had spent two years in New York, on a Broadway production. They were swopping stories, becoming great friends.

'I have so much to tell you' said John, turning towards me. 'I don't know where to begin.'

'You mean about the Sherlock Holmes mystery?' I had heard nothing about it recently. And I knew it was his reason for being here on the tour.

He nodded. 'I won't go into detail but I had a long and interesting chat with Andy.' He suddenly stopped. 'Which reminds me, has anyone seen him since yesterday?'

'I heard he was back in Edinburgh.'

'Oh.'

John was interrupted by Ted's voice booming over the microphone. 'I'm told we'll be met by a barrage of TV and the press when we arrive in Aberdeen. Prepare yourselves, especially Charles. We'll keep them to five minutes and no longer.'

'Right Ted. I guess I can handle it. Thanks for the warning' Charles said across the length of the coach.

John continued.

'Andy has the manuscript and there's a big family feud.' He stopped suddenly. 'I'm afraid I still haven't been able to see it. I would like to though.' He was now almost thinking aloud. 'I hope he's not kidding.'

'Well, why would he?'

'He's, as we thought, a tricky character. Somehow he's connected with The Deerstalker. A very dark horse.'

'So, what did you think of Glenmorchie? I said suddenly.

'A strange, strange place, it will always give me the shivers.'

'But we didn't see a vampire though I was scared that we would at one stage.'

'No. All those marks and tracks you saw were made by

193

a replica of a beast that  they used in the film.'

'And we didn't ever see the end of the film.'

'No, but we will.   I have it. I was told we can keep it.'

John lapsed into contemplative silence and the coach rolled along with a hubbub of  voices and occasional laughter.   Everyone was very happy today. We were indeed back on track.  The coach engine purred; outside the sun shone across miles and miles of  open rolling countryside, occasionally  broken up with small streams. Overhead, eagles  circled looking for their  prey.

With   glorious mountains in the background far, far away it was easy to see why people moved to live in remote cottages - and castles - away from  the urban sprawl.      There is a great aptitude for life here, I thought.

Yet it is   often in the small and simple things. And nature is  king. Not  us.

We passed through  Ballater without stopping. Someone pointed out to Charles where we had earlier seen and taken pictures of H.R.H. Prince Charles.      He was eager to hear about it all.  Yet happy to relax  quietly too.  The fact that his father, a businessman in Toronto with estates of his own, was on  the journey too, and for the first time ever in  Scotland, was an added pleasure for them both.   They often  reached over between seats and pointed at aspects of the Scottish scenery.

We were hoping to see deer  and  stag  hounds  on  the

higher mountains. And Ted had binoculars that he handed around for us all to try to see them.

I lapsed into silence, enjoying snuggling into the warmth of the seat in the coach. In truth I was still tired. It was nice to just relax without a care in the world.

Just outside the main road into Aberdeen the weather changed; storm clouds were turning the sky a dull angry purple.

We were in for some heavy rain. A few of us had macs but not everyone.

Through well mapped streets that were wide and had splendid detached rather grand houses, the coach went, keeping well within the 30 miles an hour speed limit. Many of the huge stone built houses were now turned into offices, but lit on the inside by glass chandeliers and with formal outside gardens and stone decorations.

This was no dismal, run down and tenemented narrow entry into Aberdeen. It was all classy and stylish.

Suddenly it began to pour with rain. Outside people were scuttling with umbrellas held high. The traffic lights flashed bright in the rain, reflecting as they changed colours on the wet road. We passed along a shopping area, all glittering and busy. Could this be Union Street, the main thoroughfare? I guessed it was. It was all much larger and grander than I had imagined.

As swiftly as it had become grey, then black, the low clouds parted to reveal rays of bright sunshine.

It was a strange wild sky.

'There must be a rainbow.' I said, almost to myself. Sunshine and showers. I looked in vain.

Ted swung the coach onto a massive car park and said through the microphone 'There's a fine view if ever I saw one. Aberdeen - the silver city.'

The huge municipal buildings all had turrets and looked just like castles. I gasped. The sun shone brightly through the clouds and the sky began to clear into a beautiful bright luminescent blue; the white granite buildings sparkled, 'like silver.' And then the rainbow appeared - a perfect arch of pink, blue, green and purple, like a large majestic halo.

Ted was aware that cameras were snap-snapping. Don's cine was whirring.

We all stared, entranced, stunned.

'Is that really what it's called?' someone called across the coach.

'It's also Oil City, since the oilfields in the North Sea started rolling. Thousands of international oil men work here and fly in and out, many from the States.'

'But when the sun sparkles on the granite buildings like this, in the rain, or the frost of winter, then you can see why it has always been called from way back, The Silver City.'

We were learning so much about Scotland in a thousand varied ways.

'Isn't that wonderful' I said to John beside me.

He nodded. But was really concentrating on notes he was now making.    Within minutes he would be asking serious questions  of the jewel expert.

Suddenly Ted was talking over the microphone. He had already pulled the coach to a halt.

'We're going to park here. 'The press' he laughed 'I think they've spotted us already.'

A battery of photographers,   and television cameras balancing high on the owners' shoulders appeared, as if from nowhere.  Plus a few rather pretty looking slim young female reporters.

Was this the world's press, I wondered?

Well, at least it would soon be over and we could  go off for an hour or so in Aberdeen.   It would be a short, quick visit to this fantastic and beautiful city because of our late start.

We  were out of the coach. Luckily the  sunshine was staying firm.   And  suddenly the press were asking millions of questions.

'Which of you is Bonnie Prince Charlie?' said one  TV reporter.

Charles stepped forward.

'And your father - The Old Pretender - is he here?'

Looking rather quizzical, Edward, nevertheless stepped forward when prompted.

'Brilliant. We'll have a few shots of you together.  Now where's  Jules, the guy who knew the secret room.'

Someone  half pushed and half pulled Jules forward. He

wasn't quite so sure he wanted  too much publicity. However he  finally started to chat to the press.

'And the coach driver?'

Ted grinned. 'Right here.'

'I believe you  also have a  well known  crime detective travelling with you.'

We all  stared  at each other.

I looked across at Jill, and Dolly who was  standing next to Charles.

'You're the lady from New York, who  is a descendant of Rob Roy.'

'Well, I'm a MacGregor' she said, loving this glory.

'And we're  ranchers from Texas, here  to  meet our Glasgow cousins' said  Dorothy.

Everyone joined in.

Questions were being asked. Press cameras  flashed in our eyes and whirred.   No one seemed to mind. It was very exciting.

'And the crime detective.   Where is he today?' said a girl reporter.

'Who on earth are they talking about?'

I looked at Jill. Jill looked back pulling a face.

'No one like that, I'm afraid.' said Ted adding 'We have Dr Hamish Craig a  leading  heraldry  expert and a doctor.'

Then a  girl reporter said 'Justin Delfont, that's the name. He works for,  well,  I can't tell you who' she stopped suddenly. 'Sorry, never mind.'

'Where's John?' I said to someone beside me. But no-one was listening.

I tried to catch Ted's attention. He was busy smiling for the cameras and telling the press what had happened.

I dearly hoped Ted would not talk about the jewels. And luckily everyone was so taken up with the rescue of Bonnie Prince Charlie, that no-one even asked. They were not mentioned.

John was nowhere to be seen.

I could hear Charles Edward talking to the press and being interviewed for TV. Then he introduced Gloria and told them how the film company had helped in the rescue, because Jules knew the big old historic house so well.

Gloria was terrific. She mentioned the new film. She had met most of the press the night before at the premiere in Inverness.

But she did not hog the limelight. She stepped forward to say how delighted they all were to be of any help.

And yes, she and Charles were now going to become 'very close friends.'

She looked up at him, smiled dazzlingly, Charles went a little pink. He was unused to such blatant publicity and charm. Urged on by the media he then kissed her on one cheek.

His father, once everyone had explained why he was being called The Old Pretender, then had a brief interview too. And declared it was his first visit to Aberdeen and indeed Scotland. But he would be back.

He had been treated 'like a King' He thanked everyone for contributing towards Charles' rescue, adding 'I just got on a plane and flew to Prestwick. I wasn't going to let my eldest son vanish. Not if I could help it.

'But I am mighty glad I came. I've fallen in love with the place.'

'Your eldest son?' queried one lady journalist, looking to add to the human interest story. 'Do you have others?'

'Three. All handsome bachelors! I'll bring them with me next time.'

There was laughter.

It was all a lovely, lovely story.

Jill sidled back towards me. and caught my arm.

'Were you in the pictures?'

'I think so. They took a big group picture at the start.'

'Good' she said. 'I think this is what they call the media circus.'

Luckily the press were murmuring about deadlines and vanishing as fast as they came.

'Where's John?' I said to Jill. 'Have you seen him?'

'No.'

'What was all that about someone called Justin Delfont?'

Ted was telling everyone not to get lost and that we

should meet back here on the car park in two hours.

When he joined us I said 'We seem to have lost John.'

He looked perplexed then brightened. 'I reckon he's gone to the jewellers on his own. Come on.'

He locked the coach. And we walked towards the shopping centre along a small, narrow old fashioned looking street.

We stopped before a door with steps that led down.

And sure enough John was inside. We could see someone talking to him. It was Andy, from the hotel.

He was standing behind the counter beside an elderly man who was stooped over something, concentrating. We were aware in the background of two very heavily built young men who looked as though they would be very happy to pounce on us at any moment.

'The diamonds' whispered Ted in my ear.

Sure enough the old man had an eyeglass to his left eye and was peering down.

Ted marched in. We followed.

John looked up. 'I'm glad you've come.'

The little, rather quaint man with wispy grey hair, was talking now to Andy. And Andy nodded.

'Mr Pettifer says they are genuine. These are the Dechter diamonds.'

There was an indrawn breath. It was as though we had all gasped at precisely the same moment.

'So' Andy's face lit up 'A deal is a deal.. here you are.'

He seemed to be handing John a large brown envelope.

'Come on, open it.'

John turned to the three of us, looking shocked. 'I did not think the jewels we found in the rubbish bin would be real, but just another set of fakes.'

Now Andy was speaking.

'I've given you the manuscript Mr Watson, as promised, in exchange. Of course when we first talked of it, it seemed a very long shot.'

He paused for a moment, then continued. 'But I am sad to part with the manuscript. It's a gem of another sort. Open it, take a look for yourself.'

John opened the rather faded and worn package and gingerly took it out. Old handwriting - that of Conan Doyle, he presumed - was clear and legible.

It was, he could see, titled 'The Case of the Mysterious Monster'

'As far as I am concerned this manuscript has become a family nightmare. No-one knows who owns it. And everyone assumes that they do. It has been going on for years. Give it to the Sherlock Holmes Society, that will be the best and safest place.'

Andy looked at Ted and the rest of us.

'I'm sorry if you are all losers in this. There can be no financial reward, I'm afraid.'

Ted shrugged gently.

Jill and I thought in this highly charged atmosphere that it was best to say nothing.

'You see' said Andy. 'I shall not say that these valuable

jewels have been found. They will go back where they came from, to the rightful owner, as quietly as possible, back into the vaults.'

We looked at each other.

'I think we can all keep a secret. Remember I have kept my part of the bargain. Now you must keep yours.'

'And if we decide not to do it this way' said John, looking straight at Andy.

At that the two young men moved forward. The little old man had already vanished. The young men in black tunic tops and tight leggings looked threatening.

'Sorry. There is no choice. You could say that losing the diamonds was just a terrible mistake which has now been rectified.' Andy moved forward to open the front door. 'Goodbye.'

We left the small shop, almost stumbling out, up the small wooden steps into the street outside.

'Well, that was a neat trap' said John. 'I'm sorry everyone.'

We were bemused and glad to be away.

'Let's forget all about diamonds and rewards. I don't think they were so special anyway' said Jill suddenly.

'True. We're far happier not being involved' I added.

It felt like a ton weight had been lifted.

'Come on. Let's find a lovely souvenir shop' I said to Jill. 'I just want to buy some real Scottish shortbread to take home.'

'And some tablet.' added Jill.

'What's that? Can you eat it?'

'By goodness, yes. It's delicious.'

We marched off leaving Ted and John to discuss the pro's and con's of the manuscript and the amazing scene we had just been a part of.

Later on the way home I sat beside Dolly. Ted was still insisting that we play musical chairs, except for Charles and his father, whom we regarded as our VIP guests.

'Aberdeen is wonderful' she said. 'I rang my sister from a shop here and we've ordered a beautiful cashmere outfit for her in soft rose pink. She is very slender. It will look lovely.' She was laughing and chattering. 'And, I bought some scones.. we'll have them back at the hotel - for late tea.'

I thought Ted looked tired as he counted us onto the coach.

'I'm not going to lose any of you, even if I have to chain you down' he half joked.

We drove along the A93, singing the occasional song. It had been a strange day. I thought about the tablet and the shortbread that Jill and I had bought. And Dolly's scones. And looked forward to sharing them later with a nice pot of tea.

# CHAPTER FIFTEEN

## *Back into Edinburgh*

Leaving Glenmorchie House next day was emotional. We were heading back into Edinburgh and The Deerstalker.

Charles, for whom the last three days had proved a nightmare, was upbeat.

He wanted to show his father round the capital city. And somehow find time for family research in the city archives.

Following that he now had plans to visit Culloden Moor, near Inverness, the scene of the 1746 Jacobite rebellion from which Bonnie Prince Charlie fled into lifelong exile.

Charles and I were now sitting together and talking. The coach left the grand and awe-inspiring mountains and glens. It was, for the moment, goodbye to the Highlands and the Cairnwell Pass.

'Being in that room must have been ..' I was going to say .. 'awful' but Charles interrupted.

He laughed. 'Well, an adventure. I had plenty of time to read. And to think.'

He paused for a moment. 'I've decided to set up a web site to bring all the Stuarts together. And to provide some informed Scottish history for exiles, like myself.'

'That's a very good idea.'

'I've learned a lot about my ancestors and I've some clues about my own heritage. But I have to check it out first.'

The coach was going at a good speed. The day bright, cool and only slightly windy. Perfect for travelling.

Across the aisle was Dorothy beside her husband Don. They were debating how and where to buy more cine film as they were running short. She leaned over and told me they had made arrangements to visit relatives in Glasgow tomorrow.

'We're taking the train from Waverley Station, Edinburgh. And my sister in law is meeting us.' She sounded very excited.

'Where does she live?'

'Quite near Loch Lomond - it's just beautiful and only about fifteen miles from Glasgow. We'll be back by evening.'

At the front of the coach Gloria was now seated beside Charles' father Edward. They talked and laughed a lot.

John and Dr Craig were together in the seats ahead of us. And Jill had moved to sit beside Jules.

Everyone seemed to get along fine. This was the essence of it all. As we travelled we talked, passing on information, taking on fresh ideas; widening our horizons. We would all arrive back in our own homes very much more knowledgeable, I thought.

'Is it an eight day tour?' asked Charles, suddenly.

I nodded. 'Though it feels as though we have been away for months.'

He laughed. 'So we're at The Deerstalker just for tonight'.

'Have you asked Ted about extra rooms?'

'Yes. All sorted; they have found space, thank goodness. A party of other guests were leaving today, which is very lucky. They were full up.'

I suddenly remembered that the Edinburgh Festival would still be on, in its third week. Edinburgh would be full of fun and very busy.

The fields around us began to look softer, less rugged with sheep in the fields. We were gliding down, down towards the central belt of Scotland.

Dorothy's favourite toffee-coloured, long horned cows could be seen again as we passed through the lush meadows of Perthshire.

She looked up and caught my eye. 'We've found a contact for Highland cattle. I'm going to ring them tomorrow to firm up on some prices.'

She was ever the business woman.

'Will you buy some if you can?'

She nodded eagerly. 'Yes, definitely.'

John said as he walked along the corridor. 'It's sad to be leaving the mountains.'

We were all feeling this sense of nostalgia. It would take us another two hours to get back into Edinburgh though Ted was moving the coach along smartly.

We felt like adventurers returning from the Andes. Ted detected the air of quietness and pointed out places that he thought would interest us, all along the way.

The sun shone and the clouds were high and skudding by.

Soon we were in Fife, in fact, the Kingdom of Fife, a proud title retained from the Picts, centuries ago. The splendid Forth Rail Bridge swept into view, like a huge many-legged animal.

Ted was enjoying being a tour guide as well as the driver and pointed out the small island lying under the rail bridge.

He had already mentioned that the great Andrew Carnegie, now an American legend, was born here in the small town of Dunfermline. His house is today a museum.

It was in 1848 that Andrew, a thirteen year old boy, left with his parents and family to emigrate to America and a new life.

Everyone was listening. Especially our American visitors.

Dorothy said to me 'At every turn there's so much to see and do, so much history. We'll be back to explore it all.'

As we crossed the Forth road bridge Ted's microphone

crackled into action once more.

'You've heard of    Robert Louis Stevenson. His famous adventure book,   Treasure Island, was based on this island here  on our left - or so I've been told.

'He  started telling the story to amuse his young stepson, then wrote it down.  It became a best seller.'

Everyone listened with interest.

A train  passed over  the Forth Rail Bridge.  Suddenly distances and size seemed   unreal.  The London to Inverness express with hundreds of people and dozens of coaches looked like a toy train  compared to this huge masterpiece of engineering.

Like everyone else on the coach I  was drawn  to gaze and gaze, until it had all disappeared from view.

~ ~

Thirty minutes  later, at mid-day,  we  stepped inside The Deerstalker. We were back in Edinburgh.

The first person to greet us, in the foyer, was none other than Mrs McGill.

She  was very delighted.  'I've just been reading all about you Charles.  You are  famous!'  Charles looked slightly abashed and  went pink.

Then she caught sight of Gloria.

'Oh,  wonderful,  you're back and so soon.'  She gave the  young film star a  warm hug and then turned to us as we began  crowding into busy hall.

209

'Bonnie Prince Charlie  and Gloria. This calls for a double celebration. I'm going to give a dinner party for you all tonight  and  we shall have a few  extra guests.'

With that she was off to start organising it all.

Jill looked at me.

Well, here we were, being feted again.

No-one knew what to say.  Besides we hadn't quite got the mountains and  Glenmorchie  out of our system yet.

Jill and I smiled at each other. Then we collected our cases from Ted at the coach and  made our way to our rooms.

It was pleasant;  like being home again.

I  flung open wide the casement windows in my pretty room and  looked out at the  garden. The roses and delphiniums were still blossoming; the  birds singing, the bees busy at  work.  It was all exactly as I had left it.

Was it really only a few days  ago when we had travelled North?  It seemed a lifetime.

I  reached for the  fresh orange juice  that I had brought back with me, picked up a glass and poured a refreshing drink.

The phone rang as I was idly dreaming and browsing. It was John.

'Amy. Can we meet in the  lounge  in a little bit?  I want to talk to you about the manuscript.'

He sounded excited yet serious.

'Yes, of course.'  We arranged a time.

I showered and changed into fresh clothes. Now we were back in Edinburgh, always an elegant city, I decided to dress in a matching periwinkle blue linen trouser suit and a white camisole top. It felt comfortable and smart, even though doing up the waist button quickly proved that I had put on weight.

I sighed. Remedial action would be necessary. I made a mental note to cut out second helpings at mealtimes.

John was already in the lounge. He looked trim and relaxed. He had changed into charcoal coloured slacks and wore a pale beige jersey over a blue shirt, and no tie.

He looked up. 'Have you discovered the Botanic Garden yet?'

'No.'

'Any objection if we sit on a park bench and talk there?'

'It sounds rather a good idea, surrounded by trees and flowers.'

'Exactly.'

I suspected that there was another reason too. I had noticed that John was not at all interested in plants and shrubs.

We sat down on one of the many seats. There was no-one about, except grey squirrels, seeking food.

'I want to tell you about the manuscript. It's quite remarkable' started John.

I half expected him to produce it and start to read a passage. But he didn't.

'Where is it?' I queried.

'Well' he leaned forward and smiled. 'I can't leave it at The Deerstalker. Far too many people know I have the manuscript. So I've tucked it here inside my shirt.' He tapped his chest.

'Is that safe?'

'They'd need to fight me for it first' he said with a grin.

'It's valuable then.'

He thought carefully.

'It's unique. These days such things are hard to put a value on. But let me tell you about it: a strange little tale. I can see why Conan Doyle decided not to publish.'

I listened carefully, intently.

He launched into a story about an 18 year old girl who met and fell in love with a young Highlander, while she was on holiday near Loch Ness. They eloped. Her father discovered that the man his daughter was with, was the son of a local magistrate, a devious fellow of bad reputation. So he set out in his hatred to punish the family.

John continued 'The case received a lot of press publicity because no-one could find the girl. She vanished.

'Sherlock Holmes' was called in. Conan Doyle travelled from London to Inverness, with Watson, his trusty assistant, to spend a few weeks trying to find her.

'It was early summer and another story running at the time was of Nessie, the Loch Ness Monster. Conan Doyle got to know some new friends and decided he would 'investigate' whether Nessie was just a glorious myth - or a cunning hoax. He thought it could not be real.

'He sat out in the middle of Loch Ness, once or twice all through the night, in his efforts to investigate Nessie. And he watched strange goings on. Things that made his hair stand on end!'

John stopped. And paused. 'Shall I go on..?'

'Um.. but remember I'm easily scared.'

'Let's just say he discovered - or he thought he discovered that the monster - the mysterious monster of the Highlands - was the ghoulish myth dreamed up by someone to both terrify and encourage tourists.'

'Then on September 6th 1896 Conan Doyle was in the boat on the loch, trying his hand at some fishing. Watson had by then, returned to London, fed up with this whole business and anyway there was work to be done.

'Conan Doyle reported that he saw 'the monster', a giant animal 'not a fish, mind you' but more like a long snake-like whale. It leaped and whirled and tossed and thrashed its body about, causing havoc on the loch. Conan Doyle was himself tossed into the water and had to swim for his life.

'He knew then it was no myth.'

213

'But the next day he was set upon by two fellows who made him promise never to say what he had seen. Or the whole village would be cursed.'

John stopped for a second then continued. 'They believed it and threatened Conan Doyle with violence if he ever wrote and published what he had seen. So he didn't. Far from being Sherlock Holmes, the great detective, he was petrified; and running scared.'

'And what of the girl; the one he was seeking?'

John smiled. 'Oh, the story about her is in the manuscript folder too. Quite nice really. It seems she was expecting a baby by the young Highlander and was terrified of her father.

'When she had the baby she re-appeared. By then of course she was married. And the father could do nothing.'

'As for Conan Doyle, he always intended to continue his research on Loch Ness and whenever it popped up in the Evening Standard in London - 'Nessie sighted' - as it did from time to time, it would remind him that this was one of his unresolved mysteries.

'Yet in his diary - there's a page insert about this too - he actually states that he knew the answer to the mystery. But would not reveal it, not now or ever!'

'Strong words' I said.

'One or two people have said since that perhaps he walked away from it as it would have denied his reputation. Nessie was not, after all 'a person' but merely a sea monster. And Sherlock Holmes was at the pinnacle of his career, solving crimes concerning people.'

It was fascinating to hear about it all.

'So what will you do now, with the manuscript. Take it to the Sherlock Holmes Society?'

'Yes, though I'm not sure if they'll be so delighted. They may see it as a problem.'

'Andy gave it to you. And after all your rushing around to find it.'

'Do you think I should let it quietly 'vanish' again?'

I shrugged. 'Well, you should enjoy having it and reading it. It's quite a surprising 'find'.

John smiled. 'Yes, I know. Remember what Andy said at the jewellers in Aberdeen. A curse if I take money for it.'

'Yes, but he didn't say you couldn't borrow it, as, a collector.' I stumbled for the right word.

John was troubled, I could see. He would dearly love to have this work of art; at least just for a little while.

'Alastair McDonald, the old Scotsman I met in Ballater, talked of 'a curse' too.'

'Oh, it's probably an old Highland thing, a ploy to scare you.'

John looked pensive.

'They're always talking about legends and dark deeds, and mysterious goings on. It seems to be part of the culture.' I said, hoping to cheer him a little.

'Legends and ghosts' muttered John  and as clouds began to form in the sky, we decided to walk and talk. It seemed impossible to discuss such things whilst seated. Besides we were no longer relaxed.

We walked fast.

On either side the  large  bushes  hemmed in the pathway. We were walking towards the  dramatic tropical plant house. Inside was a steamy view of lush verdant plants, all almost reaching to the glass roof. I couldn't help wondering what happens when they grow too large.

John was obviously having a battle with his conscience.

We walked in silence, hardly even noticing the pleasant surroundings.

'Look, I'm sorry to burden you with this' said John suddenly.

'Isn't that what friends are for?'

He laughed. 'Well hopefully for  sharing good things too, not just the problems.'

'You don't feel now that you are in danger' I said suddenly turning to him. 'Because of the manuscript?'

He stopped. 'How did you know?'

'Well, you said I was quite a good detective, my mind just leaps ahead' I said suddenly, then laughed, embarrassed.

John smiled.  'Yes, you are a good detective, Amy.'

He turned along another path, leading the way.

'The truth is I feel that someone at the hotel, maybe

Andy, but I don't know, will try to get the manuscript back, before we leave.'

'But he gave it to you, why would he?'

'He wanted the diamonds. He had to bargain with something. The manuscript was lying about and he knew it was important to me.'

'Aah.' I was lost in my own thoughts now.

We were heading around and out of the Royal Botanic Garden, beautiful in its serenity. I vowed to go back with Jill later in the day, as I had seen some plants and flowers that I wanted to look at again.

'So, what will you do? I mean now.'

John thought and said 'Have you heard of Justin Delfont?'

I stopped in my tracks. 'That was the man the press were asking for in Aberdeen. I meant to tell you but it slipped my mind.'

'He's MI5 or MI6 - one of those special branches - and a Sherlock Holmes fan too. He wants the manuscript. And has said so publicly.'

'Another collector?'

'And a wealthy one. He's in Scotland this week. That's why the press thought he was with us. He writes novels in his spare time. Like me, he heard of the existence of the manuscript and he wants it too.'

'You are not friends, though you both belong to the Society?'

John laughed. 'No, I should say not. I don't think he

has any. He's a strange introverted man.   Not married, not sociable, no family.  Just  gave his life to his work and  quite opinionated. He thinks the world revolves around him. And he  can be quite nasty.'

'How  would the press know he was here?'

'He's doing a book launch and likes to promote sales. He announced he would also be  trying to find the missing manuscript. It was in the Daily Telegraph  last week.   I think he's hoping that someone will come forward and offer it to him.'

It was all making sense now.

We were walking out of the  high iron ornamental gates. And a  few other visitors were about.

'What does this Justin  Delfont look like?'

'Tall, slim, in his  early 60's, wears black a lot. He always  looks formal. And he uses an umbrella like a walking stick. I  think he once had a  leg shot up, and  it gives him trouble.'

'He limps?'

'No.   He just leans on the umbrella  to ease  the weight from his right foot.'    John stopped for a while. 'He's elegant and the ladies all seem  interested in him.'

I was curious.

'And what's more he has  stayed at The Deerstalker.. I've seen his name in the guest book' added John.

'When?'

John raised both eyebrows. 'Only two weeks ago.'

'I wonder if he knows Andy?'

John smiled 'Bound to.'

He was suddenly lost deep in thought again. And we were at the front door of the hotel, a splendid glass and mahogany affair.

'It's rather a good hotel, isn't it.'

John agreed. 'I gather it received an additional new award last year for 'friendly customer service'. He was looking more relaxed now and forgetting for a moment about the manuscript he carried close to his heart.

Dolly and Jill were waving from across the road. After looking first one way and then the other, they suddenly rushed over. They seemed to be loaded with parcels and their faces were pictures of delight.

'You'll never guess where we've been' said Jill.

'Shopping..' I paused for a brief moment '..in The Royal Mile.'

'Well' said Dolly, delightedly 'How did you know?'

'She's a witch' said John, grinning. 'She deduces things. She knew Dolly wanted to go along the Royal Mile today, and she can see the piles of carrier bags.'

Everyone dissolved into gales of laughter as we entered the large foyer.

'It's the 'Holmes' influence' I said. 'I can't stop putting two and two together.'

'Time for a wee dram, I think' said John. 'After all we are on holiday.'

We all agreed and moved towards comfy chairs near the bar and John asked us what we would like and

219

proceeded to order.

Then we looked at what Jill and Dolly had bought; everything from a large white Scottie terrier toy dog with a cute tartan collar, to shortbread, postcards of Edinburgh, a Celtic silver locket, a small replica of the Forth Rail Bridge, two tartan ties, a lovely Scottish Guidebook with stunning pictures and even a small, long Loch Ness Monster in squiggly rubber.

'I couldn't decide whether to buy a length of MacGregor tartan to take home with me' said Dolly. 'I'm still thinking about that. I may go back tomorrow.'

'Oh, and we went into the Museum of Childhood, absolutely fascinating, some of the little toys and models were still working and they are a hundred or more years old. That was totally different.' said Jill. And Dolly agreed.

They also went into the famous store, The Woollen Mill in The Royal Mile. And Dolly ordered an ornate MacGregor Clan Crest, to put up on her wall.

'I shall really be the envy of my friends now' she said with a flourish.

'Just for fun, we bought these in a cake shop' said Dolly. 'Snowballs.'

'Oh, yes.' Tunnocks snowballs - small soft marshmallow round cakes covered in coconut each one wrapped in cellophane.

I smiled broadly. 'Have you tried them yet?'

'No'

'I've never seen these before' said Jill.

On the packet it read 'Tom Tunnock, 1897, the founder of Tunnock's Bakery. 'Prepared from the purest ingredients to give you the most delightful product.' Thomas Tunnock, Old Mill Road, Uddingston, Scotland'

I recalled snowballs well. And enjoying eating them. They are still hugely popular today.

'I have some stamps and must write my cards' said Jill suddenly jumping up.

Dolly agreed. 'I'd hate to arrive home in New York, before they do.'

'There's a small post office just round the corner.' said Jill. They were resolved into immediate action.

'Where is everybody else this afternoon?' asked Jill.

'Charles and Gloria and Edward have gone to the Scottish Record Office in Princes Street, to check their family history.

'Hamish, Ivy and Harry are taking a guided tour that includes the Castle. Dorothy and Don are out shopping and probably sightseeing.' I said, wondering if I had forgotten anyone.

'And John and I have just returned from the Royal Botanic Garden, near here. It's really, really lovely. We must all go over there before we leave.'

The trivialities of the afternoon, the shopping, the excitement of the city waiting to be explored, had taken over. We were all enjoying ourselves again. Even the sun was shining and the sky blue. Edinburgh was looking superb, bright, spectacular.

We sipped our drinks, thankful also for its tranquillity. Yet I had a feeling that it would not last.

'Has anyone seen Ted?' asked Jill.

We all murmured that we had not and thought that probably he was taking a well-earned break.

John finished his drink and excused himself.

'I'll be upstairs Need to catch up with some reading.'

He had politely admired the tourist mementoes and was now off to study Conan Doyle.

~ ~

Once in his room John took the manuscript from his shirt and walked over to open his case. Then something unusual caught his eye.

Lying on the bed was a large manila envelope with his name upon it. He put the manuscript safely away, tucking it under a shirt and locking the suitcase.

He hesitated then decided to open the envelope.

There was a photograph, rather faded black and white. It looked as though it had been taken long, long ago. Two men and two women were standing against a backdrop of mountains. And there were children. They all wore ski gear and looked serious. At a guess he thought it was a 1950's picture.

He started to read a note that accompanied it.

'Holmes'
You have stepped into  forbidden territory.
The family will not give up the manuscript.
Leave  it at reception tonight, before the party,
in this envelope.'


John sat down on the bed. He was  angry, yet not
surprised.  Who was it from?  There was a mark, more
like a squiggle, at the end of the hand written note.
Whoever it was did not want to be recognised.
He studied the picture.  There, surely, was  Mrs McGill
as a young woman.  She was in dark  leggings and  an
anorak and  carried skis.  A man stood beside her plus
three children.   On the far right of the picture was an
older couple, perhaps  the  parents. It  was  a  family
picture, probably taken, at a guess, on  holiday in the
Alps.
Could it really be Mrs McGill?   John thought hard. If it
was too long ago it  could be her mother.  He looked
again and saw a definite resemblance  in the  eyes and
the set of her jawline.
When he turned the picture over  it said simply.  January
1946, St Moritz; Ginny, Pere, Heinritch, Louise and the
children.
Then in scribbled, faded  handwriting  that he  could
hardly make out it said underneath 'The children's
second ski lesson'
It was signed; 'Heinritch Dechter'

John held the picture carefully. So that was it. The Dechter's. Someone was trying to tell him that Mrs McGill was part of that family. Was she a Dechter before she married? She could have been the little girl who looked about ten or twelve in the picture.

John turned ashen.

He had bargained with the diamonds. Now they wanted the manuscript as well. And they of all people knew that he had it, here in his room. And the letter proved whoever it was had access to his room.

For a second he thought of taking it to a safe deposit, lodging it into an Edinburgh bank. That would scupper them. John glanced at his watch. It was already 5pm. Every bank would be closed. He could try the police station, but how, if asked, could he explain how he came by it?

Finally he opened his suitcase, dug out the manuscript and started to read. He settled down full stretch on his bed for one hour, two hours and then three, enjoying delving into this priceless piece of Conan Doyle.

When he finally dressed and went down to the dinner party he was late. Everyone was already arriving. And John had done the only thing he could think of with the manuscript; he had tucked it into his shirt again, for safety.

# CHAPTER SIXTEEN

## *Heroes and villains*

A mounting sense of excitement swept through me. I had a feeling that tonight's dinner party was going to be dramatic. Though exactly why I felt this was so far eluding me.

Downstairs in the bar Charles and Gloria were enjoying each other's company. The delightful young American he had met was making up for all the problems he had encountered.

Jules and Dolly were part of the happy crowd having drinks with Edward and Dr Craig. And Dolly was enthusing about a book she now had on all clans, including the MacGregors and Rob Roy.

'I can go back to New York with all my MacGregor souvenirs, and the tartan I'm buying and talk at my women's lectures for hours and hours' she said in her charming New York drawl. 'I certainly know more about Rob Roy than anyone I can think of back home.'

There was a big discussion about whether they felt that Rob Roy was an outlaw, a rascal or a Robin Hood.

It was left unresolved, for the moment.

'He reminds me of one of my Tennessee uncles' laughed Dolly 'so maybe we are 'family'.

'And you'll come back again?'

'Just try stopping me!' she said with a big smile. 'I'm planning to make up a little party, about six to eight of us, including my sister. Now we know how friendly Scotland is, we'll come and have a great time. And we'll go to Balquhidder. I know exactly how to find out more about Rob Roy now.'

'Of course. He's buried there. And there's a Rob Roy museum' said Hamish Craig, joining in.

Dolly didn't need to be told twice. She had already worked it all out.


At 8pm when I phone Jill from my room to see if she was ready to go down to dinner, she said 'I'm still agonising over what to wear. A trouser suit or my party gear from Glenmorchie.'

'You mean the tartan swinging from the shoulder? Wear that. You looked great.'

'Shall I?'

'Yes. Now you've helped me make up my mind too. I'll do the same. I have a feeling it's going to be rather an unusual night, don't you?'

'I've been wondering exactly why we're being given a dinner party. Frankly I think I would prefer an early night. Bit like a command though, wasn't it.'

'I think things will happen…' I started to say.

'Oh my goodness, do you?'

'Just one of my hunches, don't mind me. I'm probably wrong.'

'John would say that you are always right. I'll see you in fifteen minutes' said Jill, hastily putting down the phone.

Looking very Scottish we went down the main staircase. People were already arriving in evening wear, the men in black ties or kilts. Already drinks were flowing in the bar.

I hoped to see faces that I knew. And sure enough there was Ted chatting and laughing with Hamish Craig, Jules and Ivy and Harry Sparrow and the rest of our party.

Ted waved his arm to beckon us over.

I was pleased to see him. And told him so.

'I went up to my room for a ten minute nap and just crashed out' he said, taking another long drink from a beer he was holding.

'I'm glad to hear it' I said. 'It's been a heavy schedule for you.'

He laughed. 'Well, exciting.'

'And different' joined in Dr Craig.

'Well, yes. No two coach trips are ever alike. I'm ready for anything.'

'Even the world's press following us around' said John, who had now joined us.

'I was going to say.. even Bonnie Prince Charlie.'

Everyone laughed.

Charles re-appeared in a splendid Stuart kilt and full Highland evening wear with a sgian dubh tucked into his sock and a sporran.

'Doesn't he look handsome' whispered Jill in my ear.

I nodded my head. 'Terrific.'

Ted was ordering drinks for us all when suddenly a new 'unknown' arrived with two other guests. He was young, tall and slim. Mrs McGill seemed delighted to see him.

Gloria appeared wearing a shimmering bright red gown. She knew the tall slim young man. It was, it seemed, none other than Alain de Leon, the Vampire's director. Soon, with Jules, they were all in animated conversation and introducing Charles.

Then Mrs McGill shepherded us into the main lounge. Glass and silver shone on the long dark mahogany table, flowers ran down the centre and tall entwined candelabras, with unlit candles, like family heirlooms, reached high towards the ceiling. It was all very grand.

My heart raced. It was more than beautiful. A sense of intrigue enveloped me. I was glad that I had suggested to Jill we wear our tartan; it seemed just perfect.

John was at my side and winked at me, tapping his chest. It could only mean one thing. The manuscript. I half smiled and nodded.

I was feeling more like Dr Watson to his    Sherlock

Holmes, than ever now.

We're in for a night of drama, I thought as he pulled a seat out for me and we sat down.

Mrs McGill at one end of the table welcomed us and then introduced Alain de Leon.

'Alain is director of Vampire of Glas Shiel'. She raised her glass. 'Here's to the success of your wonderful film, Alain. Welcome to Edinburgh.' She raised her own glass higher and drank a toast. We all followed.

'Alain is going to tell us something about the film. But first, let's begin to eat or cook will think we are not hungry.'

Everyone murmured gently. It all felt very contrived. Yet I could not think why. Perhaps I was just tired, I mused, sipping my chilled and quite perfect French white wine.

Alain de Leon was perhaps French, though he spoke perfect English. His dark eyes, dark hair and sallowness gave him an intresting artistic look. He looked animated. Mrs McGill had sat Gloria on his left side, Charles on his right side, obviously breaking her rule about men always sitting next to women round the table. Charles' father Edward sat next to Gloria.

John and I were closer to Mrs McGill and there were still spaces at table, so others were expected.

Dorothy and Don Oldenshaw arrived in the nick of time and Dorothy said quietly, as she went by 'Had a marvellous afternoon; tell you all about it later.'

A delicious rich grouse soup was served. Glasses were clinking. We were all rather more hungry than we had thought, when suddenly John said to me 'Did you see the news tonight?'

'No.'

'We're still at the centre of this storm about the money laundering and the diamonds. Did you know?'

I didn't.

'But surely they have the diamonds now?'

'They showed this hotel on television. Don't be surprised if the police arrive.'

There was movement at the end of the table as the empty chairs were being taken up. Andy appeared. He made apologies for being delayed, and sat down beside Mrs McGill. One of the guys I remembered from the jewellers shop in Aberdeen - a 'thug' - took a second seat. And then who should also arrive to take her place but Jenny, from Glenmorchie House.

John and I exchanged glances. The dinner party began to lose its air of expectancy. My senses were overwhelmed with the intensity of it all. I looked across at Dolly, opposite. She raised her eyebrows and I could see, her mind was working overtime.

When I finished my soup it was almost without appetite or hunger. A chill feeling touched my spine and lingered.

At the top of the table Alain de Leon and those around

him were however in high spirits.  Alain suddenly said
'I think we should make a film now about Bonnie
Prince Charlie with Charles as the star.'

Feet pounded the  soft carpet as everyone agreed.

He raised his glass.  'To our future star, Charles
Edward.'  He turned to Charles 'I won't let you get out
of this one.'  He paused and then said 'Gloria, you can
be Flora McDonald' and raised his glass as a toast.

'Flora McDonald?' queried Dorothy.

'The Scots lassie who took Bonnie Prince Charles to
safety 'over the sea to the isle of Skye.'  They say she
was in love with him.'

'Aaah'  Most people managed a sigh.  Gloria went pink
and Charles looked across at her, lovingly.  It was rather
like playing charades.

A variety of main course dishes arrived; beef, venison,
lamb.  And large tureens of baked vegetables and huge
colourful plates with choices of  Mediterranean salads
for  us to  help ourselves.

Three quarters through the main course Alain started to
talk.  He did not stand up.  'I expect you wonder why I
wanted to be here'  he said, his clear voice echoing
along the table.  'I have a confession to make.'

Everyone looked up.   So he had felt the strong
atmosphere pervading the room like an absent ghost.
He knew we were all on tenterhooks.

Beside me John stopped eating and put down his silver
knife and fork.

231

What was coming next, I wondered?

'It is difficult to explain with Bonnie Prince Charlie sitting here beside me, he has every reason to 'hate me' from now on.' He turned to Charles and half bowed 'I will therefore ask for his forgiveness, in advance…'

Now everyone had put their knives and forks and glasses down.

There was no sound.

'I contrived a plan - a game - because 'the Vampire film' was not doing, how you say, 'the business.' We had spent a fortune; half a million pounds, and not my own money.' He looked across the table to Mrs McGill. 'Much of it borrowed from investors such as Madame McGill.' He stood up, bowed then sat down again.

'We would not be able to pay back Madame McGill or any of the investors, if the film did not have a good box office.' He paused and took a sip of his wine.

'When I heard that Bonnie Prince Charlie was arriving at the hotel, the Glenmorchie, the very week of the launch of the film, I had a brilliant, if terrible, thought. How could I use the publicity of Bonnie Prince Charlie, whom I had never met, to help boost the film that was made at the same hotel?'

'But it all went terribly wrong.' He spread his hands in a gesture of alarm. 'Maybe you have guessed the rest.'

Charles sat silent, pensive, saying nothing.

'You used Charles to publicise the vampire film?' It was Dr Craig speaking from the far side of the table. He leapt to his feet 'That's diabolic, disgraceful !'

Alain de Leon was half slumped in his seat. 'I know. But I did not plan to have him locked in the secret room for days. That was not part of it I assure you.

'And now that I know Charles I feel very humble and I am truly sorry' he turned to Charles. 'I apologise again.'

'And did Gloria know?' said John beside me.

Everyone looked at the girl, her red hair and red dress like a flame.

'No!' Alain de Leon half shouted. 'I told no-one. It was my decision but it got out of hand.' He paused again. 'Now I have met you all and I know what you have been through I am indeed upset that I did it. This is why I have to confess.'

It was all dramatic stuff. I looked at John. There was almost nothing to say. Everyone looked stunned. Even Ted at the other end of the table, sat looking stumped for words.

We had all been duped.

Then one of the young men with Alain de Leon stood up quietly. 'I have to say that because of the press and the publicity the film is now playing to packed houses in Scotland. And has already been booked for the US.'

He stopped then before sitting down and said 'The film has been saved from massive debt. Mrs McGill can be re-assured that she will now not lose her large investment. She may even make a profit.'

As he sat down we all, as one, turned to look at Mrs McGill, who suddenly seemed to look very tiny.

'I put in £200,000' she said simply. 'And let them use Glenmorchie, our Highland hotel, for a small fee, just £500. You see, I did believe in the film and that it would help to promote our hotels, and Scotland. I thought it was a good idea.'

There was a continued silence. Most people filled up their wine glasses again. Everyone looked thoughtful.

Suddenly Mrs McGill stood up and said 'Thank you Alain. When Alain told me this, I knew I wanted him to explain to you personally.'

'As I feel your holiday has been terrible, I wish to make amends and provide a free holiday of two weeks at this hotel for each of you, to come whenever you like.

'I hope you will take this offer because I think that despite everything you have all enjoyed being here in Scotland with us.'

There were a few murmured 'thank you's' around the table.

And from somewhere in another room the lively sound of Highland reels could be heard.

I turned to John. 'Well.'

'I just hope Charles is happy with that. I think they owe him a massive payment for his inconvenience.'

Everyone was talking to their nearest table partner The music from the bar became louder and we all surprised ourselves eating the most delicious    creations    from caramel creme, strawberries with cream and meringues followed by a huge selection of cheeses.

When Mrs McGill announced that coffee and liqueurs would be served in the bar, we all began to move, almost hoping that by leaving the elegant room we could escape the atmosphere and intrigue and be able to relax again.

Alain de Leon's startling confession had at least been an honest one.

And as Gloria and Charles led the dancing, launching into a Highland reel, I turned to see Andy walking towards us.

John was beside me and said 'I've been asked to hand back the manuscript.'

'Do you have something for me?' said Andy.

'I'll discuss it if Mrs McGill is present' said John.

For a moment a frown crossed Andy's face. Then he moved into the hall. 'Follow me.'

John touched my arm as though inviting me. We walked across the wide foyer and in through a large panelled door. The room inside was part study and had books from floor to ceiling.

'Wait here and I'll bring Mrs McGill' said Andy. With that he departed.

'I need him to admit that he has received the Dechter diamonds' said John. 'I don't think he has handed them back.'

'Isn't this all dangerous?'

John nodded. 'Yes. But if Mrs McGill trusts him, as I believe she does, he will have to behave in front of her. Besides the manuscript really belongs to her too. I wonder what sort of a lie he has told her.'

Andy was now back in the entrance with Mrs McGill and closing the door behind them. Far away the Scottish music could still be heard.

Mrs McGill looked distinctly uncomfortable. 'Let's, please, all sit down' she said as though she had had enough drama for one night. She looked tired, even frail now.

Andy paced up and down.

'I've asked Mr Watson to return the manuscript to you. But he wishes to do it in person.'

Mrs McGill sat quite still for a moment.

'Let me tell you a story, a sad story Mr Watson. My husband, Bernard, was, just like you, a Sherlock Holmes enthusiast. He adored all Conan Doyle's works. Then one day when we were in Inverness, near to Loch Ness, he heard of the manuscript, The Case of the Mysterious Monster, and he set his heart upon retrieving it, for his own family archive.'

'You see he was a distant relative of Conan Doyle. So it mattered a great deal to him. We have many papers, lots of letters from Conan Doyle. They are all here, in his private study. He planned to write a new biography about the creator of the Sherlock Holmes mysteries.'

She paused. 'As you already know Conan Doyle also

worked here in this very study, writing.'

John's face began to look entranced. His eyes widened. Mrs McGill continued.

'It was about two years ago that Bernard finally got hold of the manuscript. He was told that it must never, ever be published or its contents revealed.'

She brought a hankie from her sleeve and touched her eyes. 'He did not listen... not to me .. or anyone. He said he did not believe in such ridiculous things. He said it was 'the find of the century'. Everyone wanted it. Either he would publish it or sell it, or do both.'

He took copies of the manuscript. He did not sell it but was planning to. He started to receive death threats and one day the original manuscript disappeared from this very study. Within six months he had had a stroke from which he did not recover. He could neither speak nor move. He died within the year. He was just 57 and had been fit and healthy all his life.'

Mrs McGill looked almost distraught.

'If you have the manuscript, and I believe you have, I implore you don't make the same mistake.'

John paused for a moment, obviously shaken. 'What will happen to the manuscript if I return it?'

Mrs McGill looked in control again now. 'I shall destroy it, so that it can cause no further harm.'

'And the Dechter diamonds?' John decided he would not make it too easy for Andy, who so far had said little or nothing.

'They belong to my family. I am a Dechter on my mother's side. She is Swiss. I keep them in the family vaults for collateral. I took them out to have copies made for the film and the original was never put back. They vanished.'

'Do you know who has them now?'

'The police are still looking.'

A swift glance passed from John to Andy in total disbelief. So he was right. Andy still had the diamonds. He would try to bluff it out.

'May I ask you a personal question Mrs McGill?' said John.

She nodded. 'I feel we are friends, please do.'

'Is Andy your son or a business manager?'

Mrs McGill looked taken aback. 'I have no son, Mr Watson, why do you ask?'

I could see that Andy was looking white-faced, his eyes flickering. Was he thinking of making an escape?

'He has the Dechter diamonds, ask him' said John jumping up and turning towards Andy. 'I gave them to him this morning.'

Andy was already near the door and leapt to get away.

John chased and as he did so he pulled the ill feted manuscript from his shirt and tossed it back to the study table where Mrs McGill sat. It landed before her. And she picked it up, her face emotionless.

In the foyer it was mayhem, two policemen and Alain and Charles and John were now giving chase to Andy and the jewels.  There was a scuffle as the policemen tried to take hold of Andy.  The young man held them off and made a dash for it, knocking into guests on the way.  He rushed for the front entrance and out into the street where a getaway car was waiting.

The dance music stopped.

The sound of police sirens echoed through the hotel and blue lights flashed across the wide windows.

Everyone looked stunned.  And no-one spoke in more than a whisper.  Alain and John and Charles were back in the foyer.

'What's going on?' said Jill to me.

'The police are after young Andy.'

By now Ted was at our side.  I remembered how we had confronted Andy in the jeweller's shop in Aberdeen and he had taken the diamonds from us. And the two bullies he had with him in case we said no.  And how often we had thought that he was involved in most of the dark deeds that were going on.  Now the police seemed to think so too.

'Will they catch him?' said Gloria.

'It's the diamonds isn't it' said Alain, joining us now. 'I always felt   he was totally untrustworthy but could never prove it.'

The bleep, bleep of a police mobile phone sounded across the foyer. Then a     car radio microphone: 'Heading for the castle. XJ8 to PETER, come  in. Please follow.We're giving you back-up. Over and out.'

Charles and Alain and John listened. 'Don't say they've lost him' said John. In one movement they decided they would follow too.

'We'll grab a taxi' said John. But Alain was already calling for one on his mobile phone.


It all happened so fast. One minute the Edinburgh Military Tattoo was a riot of colour and noise with Scottish regiments marching and  drums rolling; the guns were pounding as the military showed their strength to the delight of the thousands of parents, grandparents and children enjoying the spectacle: the late night  final tattoo.

The next moment police cars were on the esplanade, their blue lights flashing.

Everyone cheered. It looked like part of the show.

At first the commentator whose voice echoes loud to the spectators, said nothing. Only he knew this was nothing to do with the normal programme. Then he put through a private call. 'What on earth ..?'

He was told by the sergeant on the  ground, in pure Scottish 'I ken we'll just try  ta ignore it, sir.'

'But how?' said Commander Scott  Jackson, the commentator, a fiercely loyal Army man.

'I dinna' ken'  replied Sergeant McNeish of the Royal Scots.

The Commander decided he      would have to   say

something. 'The police cars on the esplanade. It's a routine emergency exercise' he said as dispassionately as possible while he looked with increasing horror at what was going on.

Now one car, not the police vehicle, had been abandoned near the castle gate, and a man was running towards the battlements. Three others were following. Police leapt out of their cars to join in the chase.

The audience now had their attention switched away from the military tattoo. Whatever was happening had 'grabbed them'. The Highland regiment continued to parade, cymbals clashed and pipes skirled.

A shot rang out but no-one knew if it was the police or the hunted man. Or part of the tattoo.

It was two minutes to the end of this huge military spectacle. Tonight it was being filmed and shown 'live' around the world.

Within seconds the pipes and drums of the Highlanders would wind down, the searchlights flood over Edinburgh castle, then switch low and it would be in blackness before the traditional last post was sounded and the piper stepped onto the high battlement to sound a sad lament.

Instead as the lights dimmed low and the piper began to move forward into the spotlight, there could be seen Andy astride the battlement. Charles was trying to clamber to reach him followed by Alain de Leon and two policemen.

The last post sounded as the piper continued. There was a huge gasp of shock as suddenly the young man fell from the battlements. As he did so the light picked up a cascade of glitter. It was falling from his pocket and sparkled like diamonds .... The Dechter diamonds!

The tattoo ended with most people wondering if that was all part of the show. Or not. Commander Scott Jackson knew it was not. He decided that the police would need to be told not to finish a police chase in the middle of the Edinburgh military tattoo. Whatever had possessed them?

As for the police. One of the detectives picked up the diamonds that were scattered in the long grass below the battlements. And as the crowds swept down Castle Hill, excited and exhausted by the show of military and musical prowess held under the stars, they wondered why they enjoyed it so much. Yet they did.

A police ambulance went by almost unnoticed. It was Andy on his way to intensive care at the Royal Infirmary, just a few minutes away. Charles, Alain and John were taken back by a friendly Edinburgh police driver who thanked them for their help.

They were dropped at The Deerstalker. Everyone was waiting. It had been impossible to even think of going to bed. Though Mrs McGill had retired.    Dr Craig suggested it and she was happy to do so. It had been an exhausting night. For the rest of us, we sat talking in the bar, and drinking until the early hours.

One of the newspapers arrived, the Daily Mail, and talked to Charles, John and Alain. And their photographer took pictures. They were going to have their faces spread over the morning papers, again! Heroes each of them. And Charles was still credited with the Bonnie Prince Charlie title.

When it was 2am I noticed that Charles and Gloria, both looking tired, were nevertheless dancing quietly to a slow, dreamy waltz that someone had put on from a late night radio show.

Ted said suddenly 'Shall we all have a noggin before going to bed?' And went behind the bar to pour them for us.

'That would be nice' I said. Jill, Dolly and Dorothy, indeed everyone, agreed.

Edward was chatting to Jules and a small crowd of the men, telling them adventure stories from back home in Canada. We were all quietly winding down, at last.

'Will Andy be allright?' Jill asked me.

'I gather he will. Lucky lad. Bad concussion, that's all. Though he'll find himself in jail I suspect.'

We quietly sipped our drinks. And then everyone started saying their goodnights. Tomorrow we were going home.

# CHAPTER SEVENTEEN

## *A handsome reward*

Early morning rain had drenched the flowers. When I opened the bedroom windows the sun was beginning to shine through.

Rather like a school trip that had finished I was only too aware; this was the last day.

At 8.15 my phone rang. It was Jill, asking if I was up and about.

'I can't sleep' she said, a little sadly. 'I've been up hours, packed my case and everything.'

'Shall we go for a walk in the Royal Botanic Garden?'

'That's a good idea.'

I put on navy trousers and a white top. And carried a jacket in case it was chill after the rain. It was September 3rd.

We decided to walk and talk, as we would have much sitting down on the coach to look forward to.

'Did you sleep all right?' asked Jill.

'Like a top. Probably all those late liqueurs helped' I smiled suddenly, almost to myself. 'What a night.'

'And you?'

'Yes, never heard a thing.'

'I'm really sad to be leaving, aren't you?'

Jill nodded. 'It's been incredible. I can't believe it's all over.'

'I know exactly what you mean.'

We had rounded the corner where before us stood the large tropical plant house. It was too early in the day to go in. But we admired the plants from outside. And then walked the long straight paths where flowers and shrubs blossomed on either side. Heavenly.

'It's been quite an amazing eight days.'

'I must remember to swop addresses to keep in touch.'

'Me too.'

Ahead of us I could see, of all people, John walking, now wearing his deerstalker hat, deep in thought.

If we had not said 'hi' he would not have seen us.

'Holmes, I presume' I said, feeling quite nostalgic. He jumped as though in shock.

'Sorry John, didn't mean to surprise you.'

'A million miles away' he said, adding a swift 'Hello' and then smiling.

'I'm not surprised you are preoccupied after all that went on last night.' I said. And then to Jill. 'You know we confronted Andy and that's when he made a run for it.'

'I heard something like that.'

'And John has handed the manuscript back to Mrs McGill.'

Jill was listening. And said nothing.

'What about the invite to come back again. Do you think you will?' said Jill suddenly to both of us.

John and I both looked up and said 'Yes' at the same time.

'And you?' I asked Jill.

'Yes, of course. We must plan it so when we come, we have Ted again as our driver.'

We were walking towards the large entrance gates.

'I think I feel more like breakfast, now.' Jill said with a smile.

Over breakfast of bacon, eggs, fried tomatoes, mushrooms, black pudding and hot buttered toast, we talked about the highlights and drama of the holiday.

We were drinking coffee and enjoying scones.

When John spread lots of delicious marmalade on his toast Jill said with a smile 'You know it's a Scottish 'invention'.

John grinned. 'What, marmalade? No, I didn't. How amazing!' He was looking more relaxed again.

'Dundee' said Jill. 'It's in one of the tourist guides.'

It was 9am when Ted appeared followed by Dolly and the Oldenshaws, then Charles' father, Edward.

Ted said the police were looking in at 10am with some new information for us.

'Just a two minute call. I told them it had to be quick as we're leaving at eleven.'

Mrs McGill popped her head in the door She seemed

quite refreshed and went over to John and excusing herself asked him to go through to the kitchen when he had finished his breakfast and had a minute to spare.

'I hope everyone's fine today' she added.

We all smiled, nodded and said we were.

'Good. Last night was a drama, and no mistake' she said with an amused twinkle.

I felt that everything was sliding back to normal. Soon we would step onto the coach, and the miles would begin to roll away.

John had gone into the kitchen to see Mrs McGill when who should come through the door, but Heidi, our long lost friend.

With her was a tall, handsome, well built man in his sixties, who wore a kilt.

'I've come back to say farewell. And apologise for skipping off like that.' She was sparkling and looked lovely and very smart in her eye-catching bright pink top and velvet trews.

'This is Robert ' she touched his hand 'my fiance. We knew each other when I was here 30 years ago.' They smiled happily at each other. 'And now we are to be married next month.'

It was all so emotional that I went over and gave Heidi a kiss on her right cheek. And Jill followed.

'You've read about what happened to us.'

'Yes' she laughed. 'We've been agog, haven't we, Rob?' turning to the man by her side. 'Quite celebrities now.'

Two minutes later she was off. 'Give everyone else my love' she said and waved as they left.

Ted smiled and said he would.

When John came back he said that Mrs McGill, true to her word, had destroyed the manuscript, adding that it should have been done years back. She had invited him to help her as she put it page by page into the kitchen Aga. Together they had watched it burn.

'Are you upset?' I said.

He shrugged. 'No, not really. It's probably for the best.'

Just then Edward went into the foyer to get the morning papers and brought a batch in for everyone to read.

'Are you glad that you came?' said Jill to the handsome Canadian.

He grinned. 'Yes, mighty glad. What a tale I have to tell. No-one will believe me.'

'You must take lots of newspapers home as proof.' said Ted.

He nodded as we all looked in almost disbelief at pictures of Charles, John and Alain clambering with the police upwards over the battlements at Edinburgh Castle.

As Ted and Edward and the rest of our party all settled down to eat and read the papers and have coffee, and share the excitement of the night before, I realised not for the first time, what an amazing eight  days it had been.

Ten minutes later Charles and  Gloria appeared  and joined the breakfast party.     Jules sent his regards regretting he  had  had to leave  early to get to Glasgow, as had Alain. They left cards with their phone numbers and addresses.     And  promised we would  all meet again, and soon.

We were  moving about the hotel, getting our cases into the foyer. Ted had the coach parked outside at the front and was beginning to load up,   when the police arrived.

He  was a pleasant,  smiling police officer who carried a small  leather case. And he was with a younger police assistant.

'Right, everyone.  I have some very good news' he said. 'We heard late last night from Interpol that a big reward was offered for the return of the £2 million  laundered money that, thanks to your help, we managed to  pick up at Glenmorchie  earlier this week.'

We  were  all  looking  and  listening.     What  was  he saying?

'It has  in fact led us to a route that we had tried to  tap for the last five years. The  reward  is  £ ¾ of a million in cash.'

There were  indrawn breaths  and an amazed 'Wow !'

'It's to be shared equally between everyone on the coach trip. You've  all played your part. When you went to Ballater,   we  were  able  to  go  through  the  place, properly. We set up traps that helped to confirm our suspicions.'

The police officer had something in his hand. It was a cheque, which he started to pass round.

'Now, I also want to show you all the real Dechter diamonds collected from the Edinburgh Castle esplanade, as you know, again thanks to you.'

He smiled and opened the case. The lavish jewels glittered beautifully. 'The real diamonds!' said the police officer. 'Nothing fake about these.' Everyone pushed forward to see them, their eyes wide, faces smiling. 'And there's a big reward for recovering these as well.'

Ted moved forward to speak to the police officer.

Then the policeman said 'Ted has asked if you can nominate one person to deal with all the paperwork, like bank details, so that we can divide the money up and get it out to you nice and fast'.

'I know you are leaving in about an hour. But it will be done by post within the week.'

'Any suggestions?' asked Ted to all of us.

'What about John?' said Hamish Craig. 'If he will. He's a former police detective.'

We all turned and looked at John, who seemed to be agreeing.

Hamish called out 'Don't worry, John. I'll lend a helping hand too, if you'd like me to.'

'And you are, sir?' asked the policeman.

'Dr Hamish Craig.'

John agreed and went towards the policeman.

Ted was saying that he could supply a list of the names and addresses of all members of the coach party, once we were back in London, tomorrow.

'Good. Looks as though we're all sorted.' The police officer beamed. "You've done a fine job. The Chief has asked me to say thank you. I reckon we'd like to see you back in Edinburgh again, anytime.'

Then he turned and taking the WANTED sign off the wall, handed it to Ted. 'You might like to have this as a souvenir - now that the job is completed. Have a safe journey.'

He started to put the jewels and the cheque away as we all milled about, still incredulous. Then he looked back and added with a happy grin 'Mrs McGill, these are your property once more.'

Mrs McGill had appeared and was standing behind us. She took the jewels, thanking him.

'Gosh, we can certainly afford lots of holidays in Scotland, now' said Jill, almost skipping up the stairs ahead of me.

'Let me see. I'm going to work out how much we shall get, sort of roughly.'

It all seemed like a dream. I felt I needed to pinch myself, as I had so often felt on this trip.

At 11am with much waving and many hugs for Mrs McGill we drove away from The Deerstalker. The police were leaving with her for the bank within minutes to deposit her valuable diamonds safely.

We had two extra passengers on board, Gloria and Edward.

Charles and his father had decided not to go North to Culloden but to return to Scotland in two months.

'We've booked to stay here again.' said Charles delightedly.

Ted turned the microphone on as we pulled away from the hotel.

'We'll all be back again' he said, capturing our mood.

I think we were each of us wiping a tear from our eyes or biting our lips, pretending that it had had no effect at all upon us. But knowing that it had. We were changed people.

Ted too was a winner, sharing with us the prize.

John sat at the window beside me. As we pulled away from Inverleith he gently touched my arm. 'Look. Justin Delfont, heading for the hotel.'

I caught a fleeting glimpse of the tall, gaunt man who had wanted the manuscript, too.

'Do you know, I think we have done him a favour' I said.

John nodded.

'Are you allright about it all too?'

John thought for a moment. 'Yes. In truth I am.'

As the coach went along Princes Street and out towards the A1 I looked back for a last glimpse of Edinburgh

Castle, today looking  serene and   beautiful in the morning sunshine. It was hard to imagine what had happened there only last night.

Lost in our own dreams the coach party settled down for half an hour in quiet contemplation.

Ted put some music on. It was a commercial radio station. At mid-day when the news came on  we  were amazed to hear we were  the headline.

'The  coach party  of  tourists from England, America and Canada, have been congratulated  by police for their part in capturing a ring of international thieves involved in worldwide money laundering and jewel robberies  in Scotland. One of them is Bonnie Prince Charlie from Toronto.

'They'll  receive a  reward of £1 million !'

A mighty, happy,  cheer went up and echoed all round the coach.

Then  we  settled back   and  watched the  Midlothian countryside  sweep by, almost like a dream.

At our first stop in the Borders as we changed places, Charles came to sit beside me.

'I wanted to  tell you  Amy' he said. 'Hamish is going to research my   genetic history regarding Bonnie Prince Charlie.   He's pretty knowledgeable about it all. We already think there are some major positives.'

My eyes went round and wide. 'So, you mean it could be true?'

He smiled and  looked really delighted, adding 'Gloria is

coming back to Toronto to spend a month   with us.'
'Lovely, I'm so glad.    And will you do a film with Alain?'
He nodded. 'Hope so. He says I'm a natural.'
Charles thanked me for all my   help and research, adding   'And will you come back?'
'All the time. I'm part Scottish too, with much more research  to do.'
We were all busy exchanging  home addresses now. No-one wanted to forget to  get details of those they wished to keep in touch with.
'Did you ever find out where Jenny fitted in?' I asked John  later.
'She's Andy's mother.'
'So she probably was in it 'up to her neck'.
He nodded. 'Yes.  Mrs McGill didn't know they were related. She trusted them both.' He stopped for a second. 'To be fair we think Jenny was just trying to help her wayward son. She's not  being charged with any offences.'
At our  next stop in Northumberland  Ted was enjoying a coffee with us all.  We had stopped at a motorway café, a Little Chef, just for a change.
'Thank you for everything, Ted.  We've had a great time!' said a voice over the tables.   It was Mr Jenkins.
We all joined in.   And someone led a three cheers for Ted.
When the noise stopped, a   grinning and  slightly

embarrassed Ted said 'Thank you. I have a feeling we'll all be doing this again.' He raised his coffee as a toast.

I heard someone at a nearby table say 'That's the coach party. You know, the one's with Bonnie Prince Charlie, who won all that money.'

Everyone in the café seemed to join in and they cheered. Then we were on the road again and the miles rolling by. More traffic, more chaos I thought, with almost a sigh. We sat in a motorway jam that stretched at least three miles.

'Do you know how much we shall receive?' said Jill, sitting now next to me. 'About £40,000 each. I've just worked it out.'

'Wow, that will pay for a few holidays. Shall we check with John and see if we can pass it round?'

In the end John asked Ted to put it out over the microphone. Everyone cheered again.

At the next stop I decided to ask Ted about the ghost, my ghost in armour and the man in the coach that Don had spent an hour or so on the way into Edinburgh, talking to.

Ted laughed. 'I'm a bit superstitious. I always leave a spare seat on the coach - for the ghost. When he turns up it's always a good omen.'

'You're pulling my leg.' I said, amazed.

'No.' he shook his head. 'It's just part of coach tours.

'We meet all sorts of people. And we meet ghosts.'

~ ~

Dolly was catching her flight back to New York the very next day; Dorothy and Don Oldenshaw were flying home to Texas via Glasgow to meet and say 'hi' to their cousins, having already ordered three young Highland cattle to start their own Highland herd. Charles, Edward and Gloria were off to Toronto.
We motored back through England, our heads and hearts still in the mountains.

~ ~

Jill, John and I sometimes meet in London, along with Dr Craig, and take in a concert or do a show. We're planning another trip North of the border.

When my phone rings long distance it is often Dolly calling from New York, to tell me of her latest Scottish lectures or Dorothy, in Texas, on their ranch with news of their young Highland cattle. And just for a moment we are back at Glenmorchie with Bonnie Prince Charlie and 'Holmes'. We are learning to dance a Highland reel with maybe a swathe of tartan swinging from one shoulder and with Jock, as ever, playing the bagpipes.

Born in London, after becoming a journalist Della Mason travelled to Scotland to work for the Daily Record. Much later she joined The Scotsman and became Womens' Editor and lived for many years in Edinburgh.

She has contributed to the Daily Telegraph, Daily Mail and The Times. She now lives in South East England and frequently returns to Scotland to enjoy her 'adopted' country.

To purchase a copy of this book and
receive details of forthcoming
publications
write direct to  the publishers

Travelogue Publications
PO Box 3751, Bournemouth BH1 1YJ
Dorset, England

Please send £5.99 plus p/packing of 40p
Payment by cheque to
Travelogue Publications

Applicable only in  the UK and  Ireland


Name and address  (please print clearly)

-----------------------------------------------

-----------------------------------------------

-----------------------------------------------

-----------------------------------------------

-----------------------------------------------